PRAISE FOR

Love After Life

"Here is a lucid, deftly told story of the healing power of love and the tenacity of spirit. But this is also a suspense tale with a redemptive twist — a genuine metaphysical thriller that seizes the soul and keeps you up until midnight turning the pages."
—TIM FARRINGTON, author of *The Monk Downstairs,
A Hell of Mercy*, and *California Book of the Dead*

"This beautifully plotted tale of the hapless and the sublime takes off when a clueless man has one generous, heartfelt thought. Comic pratfalls and crossed wires abound and delight until a miracle that was brewing all along comes to fruition... A fabuluous approach to an elusive and important subject." — CLIVE MATSON, author of *Let the Crazy Child Write!*

"D. Patrick Miller has done what all novelists hope to do — hook the readers in the first five pages and not let go. Wendy and her father Lucas are immediately real and vibrant characters, and it is well worth the reader's time to take their journey with them." — M.J. ROSE, NY Times best-selling author of *The Last Tiara* and *Cartier's Hope*

ALSO BY
D. PATRICK MILLER

Understanding A Course in Miracles:
The History, Message, and Legacy of a Profound Spiritual Path
(2nd Edition, FEARLESS BOOKS)

Living with Miracles:
A Common Sense Guide to *A Course in Miracles*
(TARCHER PENGUIN)

How To Be Spiritual Without Being Religious
(HAMPTON ROADS)

The Forgiveness Book
(HAMPTON ROADS)

Instructions of the Spirit
poems & intimations
(FEARLESS BOOKS)

the christ poems
communiqués of the inner life
(FEARLESS BOOKS)

LOVE AFTER LIFE

a parable of parallel realities

FEARLESS BOOKS

NAPA • CALIFORNIA

LOVE AFTER LIFE
a parable of parallel realities
THIRD EDITION
by
D. PATRICK MILLER

© 2022 D. Patrick Miller
Published by Fearless Books
PO Box 3354 • Napa CA 94558
www.fearlessbooks.com

All rights reserved. No part of this book may be reproduced in any manner whatsoever without prior permission from the publisher, except for quotations embodied in critical articles or reviews.

This is a work of fiction. Names, characters, and places incidents are either the product of the author's imagination or are used fictitiously. Any resemblance to actual events, locales, or persons living or dead, is entirely coincidental.

ISBN: 978-1-7321850-3-6

Library of Congress Control Number: 2022915375

DESIGN & TYPOGRAPHY:
D. Patrick Miller

Chapter 1

"It just isn't fair!" Lucas meant to scream, but the cry stopped in the middle of his throat just as it had stopped so many times before in his fifty years. How many times had this complaint seemed utterly justified, yet somehow too brazen to voice? *It just isn't fair,* Lucas would be ready to declare; then he would hold back, uncertain of whether he should come right out and say it like that.

This time was different, however. This time, his habitual complaint was physically submerged in his throat, drowning in a lethally impolite rush of something cold and liquid, like water. His head was swimming — literally, he realized with a deep fright. Then there was a violent thunk against his skull that reverberated far down his spine; the second thunk, he suddenly remembered, since the world had abruptly inverted and gone murky not ten seconds earlier. His spirits lifted as Lucas felt close to figuring out what was going on. There must be a good reason his feet were kicking wildly beneath him, struggling mightily to give him a decisive thrust that would finally lift him out of this — *Christ where am I?*

Thunk. The last surge upward did no more good than previous attempts. This time, in fact, Lucas felt wrenchingly sick to the very pit of his innards — *oh my god* — and then he couldn't feel his feet anymore, or anything else. Even his thinking seemed to have been jarred right out of his head. *Dammit this is it.* This last unfairness had got him; Lucas was a dead man, and he didn't even know how it had happened. He concentrated intensely, thinking that it was only fair he should know how his demise had come about. Desperately wanting to sob out loud caused Lucas to open his mouth and suck in a last, heavy, saturating draft of the river. He convulsed into stillness and began to sink.

TEN minutes earlier, Wendy Palmer had been sitting cross-legged at the end of a narrow pier extending about fifty feet into a wide, slow spot in the Russian River. Once she had been out there for a while, she had begun warming to the sunny situation; it was like having her own peninsula of private property. In fact she had already secretly named the territory around her Wendy's Island, because that's how she felt looking out over the water with her only connection to land at her back. Even if she wasn't exactly on an island, she was perfectly within her rights to think of it that way. It couldn't cause her any embarrassment as long as she never revealed it to anyone.

Wendy often worried that her childish secrets and her haunting fear of embarrassment did not befit a woman of twenty-eight years of age. On the other hand, she had a reputation for being immature and unbalanced. When this reputation was not a curse it was a refuge. She could either blame it for her relative lack of a life, or use it as a handy excuse.

Looking up from her thick paperback of *The Devil's Own*

Crosswords, Wendy sighed with petulant self-satisfaction — proud as always of her complicated emotions — and let her mind drift from the challenge of finding a five-letter synonym for *imbroglio*. Wendy's Island was the kind of thing you could tell a respectful lover, and he wouldn't think it was silly; he would think it was endearing. Weren't grown-up lovers allowed to share baby talk as part of their intimate repertoire?

Wendy sighed again, feeling excluded from grown-up love even though she had a boyfriend, more or less. She gazed unhappily down at the water, noticing that the surface ripples were looking kind of stressed as they approached the pier. So she followed them back to their unnatural source: her father Lucas rocking inelegantly back and forth in an ancient rowboat, about forty feet farther out in the dredged, lake-like spread of this part of the river.

God only knew what he was doing out there now, but his ultimate goal — getting her into that thing with him — was certainly hopeless, another of his well-intentioned but out-of-touch schemes on her behalf. Letting him lead her, a paranoid non-swimmer, this far out over the water had been crazy enough. But get into a leaky, unstable rowboat without any connections to solid earth? No way.

She watched with consternation as her father took out a paddle and clumsily began rowing the boat in a small circle, grinning brightly to show her how much fun he was having, how there was nothing to worry about and so on. Wendy smiled vaguely back at him, hoping that her big straw hat was shading her face enough to hide her disdain. She didn't want to hurt his feelings, after all. She had stopped wanting to do that in the last few years, something that her latest therapist confirmed was a sign of real growth. But she still couldn't figure out how to make him stop trying to fix her life.

This ridiculous trip to the Russian River was a perfect example. A few weeks ago Wendy had had a little crying jag about Wayne again — always Wayne — bringing herself out of it by exclaiming bitterly, "I think I'll just become a lesbian!" Her hapless father had said nothing — only pursed his lips, curtly nodded his head and, to Wendy's well-worn dismay, pulled a small notebook from his shirt pocket and jotted something down. She'd forgotten all about it until a couple weeks later, when Lucas proposed a weekend for just the two of them at a family friend's house by the river in Guerneville.

"Diane Sawyer canceled on me again," he chuckled weakly, "and I can't imagine anyone else I'd have more fun with than my own daughter."

"Fat chance" was what Wendy had wanted to say. But her therapist had warned her to watch out for those self-punishing slips of the tongue about fat. So she'd just said the usual, something like "Um, yeah, okay." By the time her dad had gone this far with one of his help-Wendy conspiracies, it was too late to point out — without hurting his feelings — that he'd made yet another colossal misreading of her real desires, not to mention her entire personality. So here they were in Guerneville because her father had gotten the nutty idea into his head that she would somehow meet a nice woman there, sometime between Saturday morning and Sunday afternoon.

In fact she'd mostly seen cute, well-mannered male couples in the town and by the water — like the two guys she'd been assiduously trying not to watch about a hundred yards out of the corner of her eye, on a little beach beneath a two-story vacation home. They'd come down to the shore about a half-hour earlier, waving and shouting "Hi!" to her and Lucas while laying out a no-doubt gourmet picnic for themselves.

It was a little while later — after Lucas had set out from the Continent in the flimsy boat and Wendy had sardonically called out "You're a dead man, Dad" and he had gamely retorted, "Oh, you'll see, little girl, soon you'll be begging to come out here with me" — when she'd next glanced over at the picnic boys to see that they had finished a pretty rapid lunch and were now in a clinch, maybe naked under the blanket wrapped incompletely around their lower halves. This had been going on for a while now, periodically distracting Wendy from her struggle with lunch.

Her therapist had convinced her that it was less important to try not to eat the stuff she really liked than to add healthy stuff to her menu, eat that first, and then see if she still wanted junk after she was "nutritionally sated." So, in between her desultory attempts at the crosswords, she had been eating handfuls of dry trail mix and staring disconsolately at a huge, cellophane-wrapped chocolate cupcake, four hundred calories at least. Picking out the peanuts first from the mix had helped, but the familiar compulsion — the magical promise of the cupcake that was somehow grander than the cake itself — was only growing stronger. Wendy wanted to cry. She knew it was really crazy to get this anxious over lunch. And lunch was only a prelude to dinner, when even bigger decisions had to be made.

There was a rattle and a splash out in the water, and Wendy looked up to see her father on his knees in the boat, reaching far over the side to retrieve his paddle. "Da-ad?" she whined in her worst sing-song voice, and he turned about immediately to face her.

"I think I've just about got the hang of this thing!" he cried.

Wendy sat up straighter, feeling a little tired, momentarily conscious of her heavy breasts, and leaned forward to squint toward her father. A sudden glare of sunlight on the water made him hard to see. She waved one arm high in the air like a beauty queen and said softly, "My father is a total loon!"

Lucas paddled out of the glare and lifted a hand to his ear, yelling "What did you say, honey?"

"I said, Write home real soon!" she shouted back. Lucas waved her off and got up on his knees again, looking for a moment as if he were praying. With a big, theatrical sigh Wendy leaned all the way back on her elbows in such a way that would allow her to peek covertly at the boys on the beach. She thought she'd caught a flash of bare buttocks when she heard a new commotion in the water, and heard her father saying, almost matter-of-factly, "Oh shit."

She sat up straight again, just in time to see something that didn't make sense: her father, Lucas Palmer, going over the side of the wildly rocking boat, his legs twisted underneath him by something she couldn't see, his head clipping the wooden rim of the rickety vessel and leaving a bloody smear just before his whole body plopped into the water. A whimper rose in Wendy's throat but stopped midway as she got unsteadily to her feet. By now her father had disappeared. She heard a muffled thunk and the boat bounced a little in the water.

"Daddy!" Wendy screamed, finally getting out a full, bloodcurdling shriek. There was another thunk and Wendy saw a hand briefly rise above the water, reaching ineffectively for the lip of the boat, then disappear. "Jesus, Daddy, I can't swim!" she shouted angrily, then spun around in a half-circle looking for help, afraid she'd lose her own balance and end up in the water too. Her eyes fell on the boys on the beach, who were just sitting up now, looking confused.

"Please!" Wendy yelled savagely at them, "my dad's out there and I can't swim! You've got to help me!"

Immediately one of the men rose from the tangle of the picnic blanket, kicking off the shorts around his feet, his long, lithe frame interrupted only by a half-erect penis jutting out from his middle. Wendy heard him bark something aggressively to his partner, something about 911. The standing man stared briefly at the pier and the water beyond, as if he were calculating distances, then pointed toward the house and yelled loudly at his still-seated friend, "Go, now!" Wendy felt tears sting her eyes as the tall man headed for the water in the fastest, most long-legged and beautiful run she had ever seen. He splashed about ten feet in before leaping into a shallow, risky, but expert dive, disappearing briefly under the surface.

Wendy turned back toward the boat, her heart in her throat, just in time to hear a third, fainter thunk, this time issuing from near the nose of the boat, driving it slightly backward in the water. Then, nothing. Wendy knew with a sick certainty that her father was sinking. She felt like an idiot standing motionless on the end of the pier, the junk of her lifestyle spread all around her: an unwrapped chocolate cupcake, her battered purse, a rumpled beach towel, a stupid book of crosswords, and trail mix that had scattered over everything when she stood up abruptly. The lone item not belonging to Wendy was an inflated inner tube her father had placed on the pier "just in case of an emergency."

Meanwhile, a strong and courageous rescuer was churning through the water toward the drifting boat, swimming as swiftly and purely as an Olympian, as though he'd long prepared for this real-life starting gun: the explosive moment that a stranger would call upon him in desperate need.

For all his speed and valor, the rescuer was now only halfway to his destination. Wendy felt a fatal point in time approaching, cruelly faster than the swimmer, and realized that she was not prepared for an actual crisis in her life.

Chapter 2

Lucas felt like a kite — lighter than air, soaring upward in a carefree, sensually zigzagging pattern, unexpectedly released from every kind of weight he'd ever known: the weight of his body, the weight of his worries, the weight of waiting on life to come across with something really good and long denied. The world was dropping beneath him like a landscape seen from a glass elevator. In fact, when he looked down he seemed to be peering through a circular lens suspended in space; all around the lens was a cloudy and infinite fog. Lucas wanted to ask someone about this peculiar circumstance, but he seemed to be alone.

At about sixty feet above terra firma the joyride slowed to a stop, and Lucas took the opportunity to survey the scene beneath him in detail. Of course he'd looked at natural topographies from the sky many times before in his career, aboard slow-flying planes and helicopters. But somehow his perception had never been so clear, so untrammeled by — what? By his own mind, Lucas realized abruptly; never before had his mind been so free of anxieties, anticipations, and both petty and large resentments that he was able to see like this, with such startling acuity. His whole being felt transparent, beatific. The piece of the world that he could see through the lens was startlingly beautiful.

Something odd was going on down below, Lucas noted in his happy dispassion. For some reason his daughter Wendy was doing a jumping dance at the end of the pier where he had left her a while ago — leaping, waving her arms, emitting a wild yelp with every other hop. Lucas was afraid she might lose her balance and topple in the water, and she'd always been terribly afraid of the water.

"Be careful there now, honey!" he called out with a laugh, bemused by the fact that he couldn't hear his own voice. He was about to try again, louder, when Wendy's dramatic gestures directed his vision over the water beyond the pier, to some bubbles surfacing next to an old wooden rowboat. Lucas felt a glimmer of concern at the sight; there was something not right about it. Then a man's head and shoulders burst through the surface of the water. The man flailed around for a moment before abruptly up-ending himself, his naked backside glistening in the mid-afternoon sun just before he slipped from view again.

Lucas glanced back at the pier to see Wendy down on her knees, her arms out to either side as if to steady herself. Then she reached for her purse, grabbed its shoulder strap and placed it between her teeth. Lucas recoiled inwardly, his happy emptiness rapidly replaced by a dark foreboding. Wendy's strap-chewing was a very bad sign, historically speaking; something awful was going on to trigger that compulsion. Lucas reluctantly returned his view to the vicinity of the boat, where the diving man was now wrestling with someone in the water. No — he was trying to hold onto someone, with one arm draped over the side of the boat and the other encircling the chest of a limp, half-bald man from the back.

But the small, empty vessel was unstable, about to tip over from the combined weight of the two men. Lucas could discern that the rescuer was furiously treading water to keep the other man afloat. Then he shouted something and Lucas saw Wendy react by scrambling to her feet, looking desperately around her before grabbing the inner tube Lucas had put near the end of the pier to reassure her. She did an awkward but rapid spin with it, as if she were heaving a shotput, slinging the tube with a ferocious accuracy to within fifteen feet of the two men in the water. The swimmer abandoned the rowboat and dog-paddled over to the tube, hauling the limp man's torso out of the water and laying it across the circle of rubber with surprising efficiency. From there it was no more than half a minute before the swimmer had pushed the tube over to Wendy, scrambled onto the pier with Wendy's help, lifted the limp man out of the water and laid him out flat.

Without knowing how he did it, Lucas telescoped his vision nearer the surface of the pier — as if he were only ten feet above the scene — and noticed with mild surprise that the man who had been pulled from the water was himself, looking soaked inside and out, insensible and blue in the face except for a messy redness on his right temple. Strangely, the deep concern that had arisen when Wendy started chewing her strap now subsided; Lucas felt more confused than disturbed.

There was something going on that hadn't quite registered; he wasn't "getting it," as Wendy always complained. Perhaps the swimmer was confused too, because Lucas noticed that he was scratching his head and looking around uncertainly. Then he seemed to make up his mind, assertively turning the head of Lucas' body to one side and beginning to push roughly on his chest. Some water dribbled, then bubbled abundantly out the mouth. After two or three rounds of this, the man who was trying to revive Lucas sat back on his haunches and said something to Wendy who answered "What?" and then slowly, wonderingly handed the man a cupcake. Lucas would have wondered what *that* was about had his vision not speedily, sickeningly reverted to its far perspective, then faded along with the mystical lens into the surrounding foggy blankness — just as he *got it*. He was no longer uncomprehending of why he was voiceless when he said to himself in amazement, "Oh my."

WENDY couldn't fathom why her father's naked rescuer wanted the chocolate cupcake, but he'd been so perfect and commanding thus far that she handed it to him without hesitation. He ripped one of its cellophane seams so violently that the cake popped out of the package, rolled off the pier and plopped into the water within seconds. Even in her distress, Wendy felt a pang of loss and then a prick of self-judgment as she watched the cupcake bobbing along its maiden and final voyage.

Then her attention returned to the urgent doings of the rescuer. With one hand he expertly forced open her father's jaws; with the other he placed part of the cellophane wrapper over the mouth, stretching it tight between thumb and forefinger. Then he punched a hole through the wrapper with two fingers of his other hand, and leaned over to start breathing for Lucas.

"Wow," Wendy sighed audibly, stunned nearly as much by the rescuer's presence of mind as her father's critical situation. She felt an urge to cry out "thank you!" but just as suddenly realized that saying anything would be premature, perhaps even dangerously distracting. So she kept silent, her hands fluttering uselessly in her lap as she sat on her haunches and watched the blond, muscular young man before her go through the cycles of CPR in a steady, confident rhythm. Panicky and engrossed, she was slow to register thudding footsteps behind her on the pier.

Now Wendy whirled around and saw the rescuer's beach companion, a dark, wiry guy wearing boxer shorts, racing toward her. He stopped short as he came close and dropped to his knees, gasping. "I called 911. They're on the way," he blurted.

Hearing "911" chilled Wendy to the core and she desperately grabbed the strap of her purse, returning its leathery, moist midsection to the reassuring clench of her teeth. Then Wendy began to sob out loud, overwhelmed by her helplessness, by the manic turn of events that had just overtaken her, and most of all by the dumb inertness of her father — who only rocked slightly in response to his rescuer's work. The wiry man got up and hopped around Wendy only to drop to his knees beside his companion, asking nervously, "What do you think, Cal?"

The taller, naked man sat up with a huge gasp and immediately resumed pushing on Lucas' chest, his breathless speech interrupted by rhythmic grunts of effort. "I don't know. Can't — can't get any response. Don't know... how long he was under."

Wendy spit the strap from her mouth and wiped her eyes, stifling a moan. "Just a few minutes?" she offered helpfully, newly frightened by the wiry man's widening eyes.

"Minutes?!" he exclaimed.

Cal sat up again and looked hard at Wendy, his face grim. "Really?" he added.

"Oh, I don't know," Wendy whined defensively, as if she'd just been caught in a lie. "Less than that, I guess. Probably less! I heard him say something, and when I looked up he was falling in the water. He hit his head on the boat and went under. Then

I yelled for you guys."

Cal and his friend glanced at each other worriedly. "I think I got out there in less than a minute," Cal said before bending over the body again. When he had forcefully breathed into Lucas three more times through the cellophane, Cal sat up again and said, "Think you could get me some pants, Tom?" His voice was raspy with exhaustion.

"Oh, right!" Tom exclaimed and bounded down the pier toward the shore.

"And some blankets!" Cal shouted after him, as Wendy stared disconsolately at her motionless father, her scattery panic solidifying into dark dread. After a few seconds she registered the floating, far-off call of a siren. For no reason she suddenly remembered sitting in front of her therapist-before-last, a big bearded fellow who hardly said anything during the four months that she saw him. In their last session, she had complained that she felt like she wasn't living her real life — as if it were lost somewhere, the same way her favorite books often got lost in the clutter of her room.

Wendy remembered getting emotional: "Where is my real life? Where do I find it?" she had cried out.

The therapist had calmly replied, "I can't answer that, Wendy. Where do you think you'll find your real life?"

She always hated counselors who threw back her questions that way; if she knew the answers, she wouldn't be asking questions in the first place, right? So she didn't see Dr. Silent Treatment again.

Now, as the whoop of the siren grew steadily louder, Wendy had the strangest feeling that her real life was racing toward her. And she didn't like the sound of it.

CHAPTER 3

FLORA appeared in the middle of nowhere, her fuzzy bright aura of strawberry pink dispersing into the translucent whiteness all around her at a distance of about two and a half feet. She held one hand out toward Lucas and displayed the bittersweet smile he remembered so clearly from the last year of her illness. As Lucas advanced toward his wife, he tried to remember something profound that he'd realized only moments before. But the substance of the big thought was gone, leaving only the tantalizing afterhint of an escaped dream.

His mind was working like an erratic flashlight, irregularly illuminating whatever was immediately in front of him but otherwise leaving him completely in the dark. Though she was dead, Flora glowed with a reassuring constancy. Lucas decided to focus on her instead of his own intermittent consciousness. As he drew near, Flora spoke to him with a slow and distinct enunciation, her smile unchanging: "Welcome here, Lucas. Love surrounds you and would always have you come home. But you may not be prepared. Follow me."

Her tone was so theatrical that Lucas wondered if Flora was trying out lines from one of her embarrassing plays. Yet her authority was unquestionable and Lucas followed her as he was told, through the foggy whiteness into a deeper whiteness, as if they were trailblazing through a cloud. Shortly they broke through the formless mist. Lucas found himself standing atop the back row of a huge amphitheater, plushly carpeted and upholstered in still more shades of white, facing a beige stage and a huge rectangular movie screen.

At least Lucas thought it was a screen, but as he peered at it more intently it took on the appearance of a great flag, reminiscent of the Stars and Stripes — but with pulsating silver lights where the stars should be, and slowly undulating, flattened-out sine waves replacing the stripes. When Lucas blinked there seemed to be fishlike shapes leaping like salmon between the waves, but then these ghostly images took on other indistinct shapes. From the seats to the flag to the sky above, the color spectrum varied no more than cream to silver to vanilla; the white-out effect was getting tiresome. Lucas looked longingly at the rows of seats before him and thought about how nice it would be to spread out in one of them and take a long nap. But Flora suddenly poked him in the side with a short wand, then pointed toward the center of the amphitheater.

"Go there and wait," she said sternly. When Lucas turned to look at her, she softened her tone. "This is your show, honey. You can't fall asleep now."

"What do you mean, my show?" Lucas replied, but Flora had vanished into a swirl of glowing snow. A brief fizz followed her disappearance. Lucas turned back to face the stage and flag. Feeling exquisitely alone once more, he shrugged his shoulders and began stepping noiselessly down the soft stairs toward the section of seats his late wife had indicated.

WENDY couldn't bear to watch the paramedics work on her father after they briefly quizzed her and Cal on the accident. With a complete loss of reserve she had simply collapsed against her father's tall rescuer, inducing him to put a strong arm around her for support. She worried for a second that she might crush the erection she had seen on Cal when he first stood up, but of course it was long gone. For about fifteen seconds she pondered the hydraulics of erections — what made them go up and down? — with her eyes wide open and blinking frequently at the hair on Cal's chest.

Then she remembered her awful predicament and began to weep again. Without paying attention to his words, she could hear Cal speaking through his chest, still giving directions to his partner or perhaps making efficient suggestions to the paramedics. Thank God there had been someone to take charge of this situation from the very beginning . . .

"We've got something!" barked a voice behind Wendy, and she gingerly rotated her head to peek at the paramedics. She saw one of her father's legs jerk and heard him make a sound somewhere between belching and vomiting. At least they weren't pounding on her father's chest anymore, which they'd been doing far more violently than Cal. The paramedic who had been pounding was a muscular woman with a severe haircut, perhaps the type of woman her father had hoped to set her up with. Wendy bit her lip and watched the woman pry open her dad's left eye with two fingers, then put her ear at his mouth. "Got something," she repeated victoriously, winking at Cal instead of Wendy. "Not much. He's way under."

The other paramedic, a tall lifeguard type who looked crisp in his red-trimmed uniform, squinted at his partner and pulled a radio from his belt holster. "We can't handle this locally," he announced. "Let's medi-vac him to Memorial in Santa Rosa. There's no time to spare."

"Roger," said the woman crouching over Lucas even though she was nowhere near a radio. Then she whacked the body again with a two-handed fist. Wendy loosened her hold on Cal just enough to look up at his face.

She wanted to see if he too thought the paramedic was weird, but Cal was scanning the scene as if to spot the next emergency. Once again Wendy closed her eyes and nestled against his chest, happy to stay there until given something to do. When she felt a tap on her shoulder, she opened her eyes to find the handsome paramedic regarding her earnestly, shaking his radio before her eyes like a maraca.

"Miss, your father needs more than we can do for him at the local clinic, and he needs it real soon. I'm calling in a helicopter to fly him to Memorial Hospital in Santa Rosa." Then he scanned the full length of her body before adding in an embarrassed tone, "You can fly in with him, I think."

"Oh my God, *no*," she blurted before she could stop herself, causing the paramedic to blink with surprise. The very thought of ascending rapidly into the sky made her weak in the knees, causing her to sag a little more against Cal. "I'll die," she added convincingly. "I'll just die."

The paramedic shrugged his shoulders helplessly and then raised his eyes to Cal, who responded without hesitation. "I'll fly in with him," Cal said confidently. "My partner can drive Miss, uh —"

"Wendy," Wendy said helpfully.

"Wendy to the hospital," Cal concluded. Then he looked wisely down into Wendy's face and said warmly, "Don't you worry. I'll make sure your dad hangs on til you get there. He'll probably be up and talking by the time you and Tom arrive."

A TV image of Lucas sitting up in a hospital bed, surrounded by hundreds of flowers and chatting happily with Cal, their new-found family friend, blossomed vividly in Wendy's mind and made her gasp out loud with gratitude. "Oh, thank you so much," she cried, joyfully aware of her feet being on the ground and staying there. She beamed happily at the paramedic, feeling oddly like she'd won some kind of prize. Beyond the paramedics and her father, Wendy saw Cal's partner Tom lifting both arms helplessly into the air. He was glaring at Cal and showing his teeth like a hissing cat, but making no sound.

AFTER a few minutes in his amphitheater seat, Lucas decided that he had never known a more comfortable chair. "This is heaven," he murmured, marveling at the weightless feeling that made him feel a part of the entire arena, extending even to the indistinct vastness beyond it. As a geographer, he was acutely aware that he was in a place without borders or boundaries, characterized by a luminous sameness that would be futile to survey. He wondered if he was early or late for the next show to take place before the glowing flag, still swimming with shape shifters, that hung without visible means of support just above and behind the stage.

He did not have long to wonder. Faint footsteps soon issued from the back of the stage, and Lucas watched with astonishment as a black-helmeted figure in a deep green uniform rose into view. A disembodied voice firmly commanded, "Ten-hut!" Lucas instinctively straightened in his seat, a secret thrill rising in his breast. The amphitheater remained empty except for Lucas and the imposing figure on stage, which was now standing impassively in a stiff salute. The uncompromising darkness of the soldier's dress was interrupted only by a small sea of silver and gold medals on one side of his chest and a wide, blood-red ribbon crossing from the other side.

The implicit command of the figure's salute finally registered with Lucas. He scrambled to his feet, raising one hand to his forehead as he realized with acute embarrassment that he didn't know exactly how to salute; he'd had a college deferment from the draft during Vietnam. He did his best, which must have been enough. The military man answered with a curt drop of his own arm and gruffly barked, "As you were men." His tone suggested that he might be issuing a statement of fact as much as an order.

Lucas dropped back into his seat with a growing astonishment. The strange, displaced placidity of the last hour or so was changing into a too-good-to-be-true gladness, for the voice he had just heard was clearly that of the actor, George C. Scott. And that meant Lucas was finally in the presence of the man he had always revered no matter how much his wife ridiculed him for it: old "Blood and Guts," General George S. Patton, the last true hero who spoke his mind.

Lucas knew the forthcoming address to the troops by heart. In the company of his best friend, he had watched this opening of the movie "Patton" countless times. To Lucas, the actor and the general were one and the same — and the cinematic speech about how Americans loved to fight, how they could never lose a war because the mere idea of losing was so hateful, how they would go through the Hun bastards "like crap through a goose" — this speech was gospel, an anthem for Lucas' real life had he ever summoned the gumption to live it.

In this strange place, there could be no better reality unfolding before him. The only question was whether he should listen intently to the speech once more, now that it was about to be delivered to him in person, or repeat it along with the General.

But something was not right: the General wasn't beginning the speech. He merely stood on stage, flicking his short whip against his ceremonial leggings, his jaw thrust forward and his eyes seeming to bore deep into Lucas even at the distance between them. He seemed to be waiting for something. Lucas felt suddenly inadequate, as if he didn't really belong in this scene after all. His eyes were riveted on the figure of darkness bristling in the ocean of white, but he wished that he could look away. His heart fluttered, he could not feel his limbs, and he was abruptly paralyzed with fright.

Chapter 4

WENDY shifted once more in her seat, as much as the cramped quarters of the ancient but exquisitely maintained Volkswagen bug would allow. Finally she found a position to sit still in, tilted toward the door, her face almost pressed against the passenger's side window. She realized there might be no way to feel comfortable, given the circumstances. After all, she was on an emergency trip to the hospital with a total stranger, and she might never see her father alive again.

Outside the window the lush greenery of the Sonoma County hills and vineyards sped by, adding an unexpected pleasure to the roller-coaster of emotions Wendy felt inside. The sun-dappled scene was a reminder that a vast miraculous world existed beyond her own immediate concerns — a world she usually failed to notice, but that now surrounded her with a luminous insistence. Then the car hit a bump, and Wendy shrank back inside her anxiety.

There was no one to turn to for help but Tom, looking grim and perhaps hostile, hunching forward over the steering wheel and gunning the bug to its noisy limit. He had hardly said a word in the fifteen minutes since they raced to the car at Tom and Cal's river house, the thrumbeat of a descending helicopter becoming audible above them as they distractedly threw her purse and his backpack into the rear seat and then sped away. Wendy had almost asked if he was sure of the route to the hospital, hastily outlined by the butch paramedic. But Wendy had felt too embarrassed, as if she were merely an unwanted guest who shouldn't make impolite inquiries. Now she needed to certify that she had an ally.

"Tom," she ventured in a quaking voice, "I appreciate this so much. I really do. I just can't fly anywhere, even if..." *even if my father is dying?!* she continued silently, feeling a cold wave of chagrin pass through her.

"Yeah," Tom replied with a cursory tilt of his head in Wendy's direction. "That's okay. We'll get there soon."

"This is a really nice car!" Wendy exclaimed before she knew what was coming out of her mouth. "It looks almost new."

"Right," Tom muttered ruefully. "If Cal put as much time into me, I'd look spiffy too."

Something about her driver's wry tone of voice struck Wendy as awesomely funny, and she let loose a belly-laugh that shook the car, causing Tom to veer momentarily over the narrow road's center line. When he regained control he looked over at Wendy with a half-smile, his tone turning softer and curious: "What? What'd I say?"

Wendy grabbed a dashboard handle with one hand to steady herself, and wiped a tear from the corner of her eye with the other; her laughter subsided to a chuckle. "Oh, I don't know," she confessed. "That's just so out there, saying something like that. Is Cal really into cars?"

"Ca-aal," Tom replied with a huge sigh, as if he had been waiting for an opportunity to comment, "is into *every little thing*, if you know what I mean. Spotless silverware, shined shoes, spice jars in alphabetical order. He does everything perfectly, and he tries to preserve things for-fucking-ever. Excuse my French, but — like this ridiculous old car, you know? It was with Cal before me and you can be damn sure it will be with Cal when I'm gone."

"When you're... gone?" Wendy hesitated, unsure of how much she wanted to know, yet grateful for a change of subject.

Tom reached over and touched her arm softly with four fingers together, the first really gay thing Wendy had noticed Tom or Cal doing since whatever they had been doing under the blanket by the riverside. "Oh, honey, I'm sorry," he cooed. "I'm being just awful. Here you've got real trouble and I'm complaining about my boyfriend. It's just that — well, this is a make-it-or-break-it weekend for Cal and me. We're trying to patch things up."

"Oh God, I'm sorry!" Wendy blurted. "That's really important! My dad and I, we were just . . . oh, I don't know what we were doing here," Wendy said disconsolately, turning her face away to rest against the cool glass of her window. "He was trying to get me into that stupid boat."

And then, as the enormity and absurdity of her predicament mixed within her like two volatile explosives, Wendy shuddered and burst forth with a mighty wail. The car swerved left again. Tom corrected by steering hard to the right while casting a nervous glance at his passenger, then scanned the road ahead and began slowing the car. Soon it drifted off the pavement onto a gravel clearing and came to a stop in front of a small café. As soon as he could get one hand free, Tom patted Wendy awkwardly on the shoulder and murmured "There, there." Her initial cry had shortly been muffled into a moan by the clamping of her teeth onto her purse strap. Tom scowled briefly at the dampness of the leather, then took a deep breath to compose himself.

"Let's stop for just a couple minutes, okay? I need to go to the bathroom and make certain we're on the right road. I mean, I think we are but I wouldn't want to get us lost." Trying to keep his voice as steady as possible, Tom immediately regretted the last disclaimer. He didn't want to spark yet another dramatic reaction from his unpredictable passenger.

But Wendy seemed freshly pacified, even happy at Tom's suggestion. She removed the purse strap from her mouth and deliberately wiped both sides of it against her black slacks, then sniffled and straightened her back against the seat. "Great," she smiled wanly, turning with red-rimmed eyes to face Tom. "I could really use a coffee break."

LUCAS turned this way and that in his plush seat, frantically trying to avoid the open-handed blows of the General, who now stood astride him, looming over the seat. Patton seemed to have flown instantly from his perch onstage into this terrifying proximity; his testy silence of a few moments earlier had abruptly transformed into crude insults. "You sorry, mealy-mouthed sonuvabitch," Patton thundered, "you think you're the only soldier in this man's army who's afraid to die?"

"N-no, sir," Lucas volunteered with all the humility of an eighteen-year-old conscript, wondering when he had said anything about being afraid of death. *Thwhack!* The General's broad palm met Lucas' cheek full-on for the fourth or fifth time, but with the same curious effect as before: an initial sting that faded abruptly into a neutral reverberation, as if his flesh had metamorphosed into nerveless gelatin. It briefly occurred to

Lucas that the General could not hurt him if he thought he couldn't be hurt. But the idea was so novel and strange that he couldn't grasp it in the middle of being violently abused.

"You make me sick," Patton continued with a sneer, pausing in his slapping attack long enough to stick both fists on his hips and boot the underside of Lucas' seat. "I should kick your sorry ass right out of this hallowed place. You don't belong here with all the brave young fighters who have sacrificed themselves for the Vision."

Now Lucas was utterly confused. He had seen no one in this strange place but himself, Flora, and the General, who wasn't making sense. "The Vision, sir?" he inquired weakly. "I don't think I understand."

"Don't question me, you cowardly sack of shit!" Patton boomed, his face instantly turning a bloody shade of red that matched the ceremonial ribbon across his chest. Lucas was beginning to feel as if he were in the middle of a bizarre cartoon. The General was literally shaking with rage, his right hand unbuttoning the holster of one of his pearl-handled revolvers. Lucas raised both hands to ward him off, but in a flash Patton had gotten his weapon free and shoved it roughly into Lucas' mouth, which had fallen open to issue a cry of horror. Instead of his own shriek, Lucas heard a faint click inside his cranium.

Then a magnificent blast blew his mind open, shattering all perceptions of himself, the amphitheater, and the all-white territory he had arrived in not long before. As his consciousness came apart in a vast blackness, countless fragments of self-awareness speeding off like galaxies racing in all directions from a big bang, Lucas could just barely hear, far beneath him, the General's refrain as he holstered his smoking gun: "Little piss-ant coward makes me *sick*."

BECAUSE they were in a hurry, Wendy went ahead and ordered for herself while Tom was in the bathroom inside the bohemian Midwoods Café. Given the tense situation, she thought she was probably hungry — or soon would be — and the devil's food cake under the plastic cover on the counter looked inviting. It would make up for the cupcake that had rolled off the pier; if she couldn't repair the big accident that had befallen her, at least she could compensate for a small one. One of her therapists used to say, "Moderation in all things, including moderation." Wendy took this to mean that there were certain extreme situations in which she could ease up on all her self-improvement guidelines. And if this wasn't an extreme situation, what was? For once her conscience could be clear about an indulgence.

A young slender waitress with dark braided hair trailing past her waist was pouring Wendy's coffee when Tom arrived to take a seat. "Coffee for you too?" she asked warmly, and Tom gazed up at her with what Wendy thought was a lost look.

"Oh no, I really shouldn't," he demurred. "I get all rattly and start speaking in tongues."

Wendy raised her eyebrows as the girl, perhaps twenty-two, laughed and set the red-rimmed coffeepot on the table. "Really? I'd like to see that. Come on, you can have decaf. It's fresh mocha java."

"Oh, dear," Tom sighed. "You really are a temptress." Wendy wondered if Tom was flirting; she knew a gay guy who said he liked to "test the waters" with females every once in a while. Tom did reach out and touch the girl's forearm, saying, "All right then, let's take a chance. We're in an emergency and need to make some time on the road. But forget the decaf. Get me the real stuff, okay?"

The girl said "Sure" and laughed while throwing her head back in such an appealing way that Wendy hated her for a second, then felt bad about it. So she called out "Thanks!" as the waitress went for the other coffeepot, drawing a quizzical look from Tom.

"I meant thanks for helping us in our emergency," Wendy explained nervously, to which Tom only shrugged his shoulders. When the girl returned and poured his coffee, Tom quickly confirmed with her that they were on the right road to Santa Rosa, with about twenty minutes to go. Lingering at the table in the otherwise empty room, the waitress then volunteered unnecessary information about avoiding turn-off roads that had been washed out in last winter's flood. Then she and Tom seemed locked in conversation about the seasonal ups and downs of the Russian River.

Wendy methodically ate her way through her cake in a moody silence, noticing that Tom went through two cups of real coffee in just a few minutes, rapidly becoming louder and more talkative. When Wendy finished eating she became anxious about the time, but she couldn't figure out a way to break into the ongoing conversation. So she started glaring directly at the young waitress, which would normally be a terrible thing to do. Considering the circumstances, Wendy decided this too was excusable.

Within half a minute the strategy paid off, as the young woman began shifting her eyes between Tom and Wendy with increasing frequency, rocking on her feet a little. Finally she blurted, "Look, I have to check something in the kitchen," then turned and walked off in the middle of a chatty aside by Tom. In reaction he only blinked, childlike, then grabbed a saltshaker from the far side of the table and began twirling it around, making an annoying clatter.

Wendy gathered her purse into her lap and said, "Tom? I guess we should get going now?"

"Oh?" he replied with a strange blankness.

"Because of my father!" Wendy added insistently.

"Your father..." Tom murmured vacantly, the saltshaker falling on its side between his hands.

Now Wendy felt righteously upset. "Yes, my father! He's going to be at the hospital, remember? We have to get there right away!"

Tom made no reply. It seemed that Wendy's concern was not registering with him. His eyes slowly traveled upward, as if he had found something in the far corner of the restaurant to look at. Wendy twisted in her seat to check it out, but saw nothing. When she looked at Tom again his eyes had a strange glaze over them. His mouth was working silently as if he were praying, but no sound came out.

Then a small boy spoke. At first Wendy could not believe the sound coming out of Tom's throat. "I see him! I see him!" exclaimed the high, small voice.

"See who?" Wendy asked automatically, a chill running over her arms.

"I see your father," the voice continued. "He's scared. He's with a bad man who's scaring him."

"He is?" Wendy asked, feeling both spooked and awestruck.

"Uh-huh," the child-Tom innocently replied. "But it's just a show in a big theater. The bad man can't really hurt him. The angel is there too."

"The angel?" Wendy asked. "What kind of angel?"

"I don't know," the voice replied with confusion, as if the question were too difficult. "But she's nice. She has a name like...

like flowers."

Wendy's eyes widened. "Flora," she responded with certainty. "You mean my mother is there too?"

Tom's mouth worked soundlessly again for a few seconds before the child spoke for the last time. "She says, *Wendy, listen. Things will happen very fast now.*"

Wendy shivered and pushed herself back against her seat as if she'd been threatened at gunpoint. By now the waitress had reappeared but stood transfixed a few feet away, with the coffeepot held motionless in midair and her mouth dropped half-open, staring distractedly at Tom.

A silent, seemingly timeless moment passed before he dropped his robotic gaze, then rapidly shifted his eyes from Wendy to the waitress and back again before speaking in his normal voice: "Uh-oh." He chuckled apologetically while rising from his seat and added, "No more of that stuff for me, honey. We've gotta hit the road."

Chapter 5

"Well, *that* was certainly premature," Flora said sardonically, causing Lucas to wonder not only what she meant, but exactly how he was hearing her. He seemed to be listening from a thousand different places, places he had landed after falling a long way. He was resting on hillocks, in hollows, alongside a creek of bright water, and even in a few treetops waving rhythmically with the breeze. He was everywhere at once and nowhere in particular, which explained why he could see Flora from all his vantage points simultaneously. She was stepping purposefully over an idyllic landscape with a huge, open flower basket hooked over one arm, picking up fist-sized, blue-white diamonds here and there.

Every time one of the diamonds landed in the basket, Lucas could hear a glassy clink as it collided with the other jewels. Soon Lucas realized that he was in the basket too, looking up at his wife carrying out this peculiar harvest. His sense of self was slightly stronger within the basket than anywhere else, growing by a tiny degree every time Flora added another diamond to the collection. It seemed that the diamonds were every tiny part of him, yet inside each one there was somehow the whole of him. Lucas couldn't figure it out.

"Yes, it's very complicated," Flora explained patiently, as if he had asked her a question. "Take it from me, you weren't ready to be dismembered yet. There's a lot of work to be done and we don't have much time."

Lucas felt three clinks simultaneously. Now he could actually feel himself swaying in the basket, hearing the rapid swish of Flora's long dress in the field grasses more clearly than he heard the water in the creek or the wind in the trees. She was working quickly; Lucas was impressed, as he had always been, by his wife's industriousness. Like a baby in a swinging cradle he let himself be soothed by the motions of her walk and her work, this magical recollection of his shattered wholeness.

WENDY felt hugely relieved when Tom yanked the steering wheel of the VW to turn into the parking lot of Santa Rosa Memorial Hospital. The ride from the café had been an absolute horror, the least part of it being the excessive speeds Tom had reached.

The worst part was that he talked and sang loudly the whole time, while not addressing a single coherent word to her. Mostly he spoke in his normal voice, but sometimes it switched as it had in the café, and then Wendy listened intently for the return of the little-boy voice with information about her father. She heard it only once, yelping "Oh no!" causing Wendy to ask "What? What?" to no avail. Instead of replying Tom had punched the radio on and begun singing along with whatever he heard. A couple minutes later, he began speaking fake Latin in a basso profundo tone, ending half a minute later with the words "*Ipso dipso flipso factotum!*" followed by maniacal laughter. Then he turned to glare spitefully at her, and Wendy tried to shrink in her seat to escape his attention.

Perhaps she succeeded, because Tom punched the radio again and began harmonizing with surprising accuracy to one of those Eagles songs that always seems to be on the radio when one is traveling. Wendy did not try to connect with Tom again. She kept her eyes closed as much as possible to ignore the high-speed motion of the tiny automobile, and vaguely prayed for safe delivery.

When the car came to a stop Wendy bolted for the sliding glass doors of the hospital, briefly muttering "Thanks" to her driver. He was now humming along with a schmaltzy Kenny G tune, his eyes moist and his hands gripping the steering wheel with white knuckles. Wendy could already recognize Cal's tall, lithe frame leaning over a counter inside the building, a welcome sight causing her to break into an open run. She barely noticed the air-conditioned coolness of the hospital before crashing awkwardly into Cal's side, exclaiming "Oh my God!"— whether from this mini-collision or the harrowing ride she had just escaped, she wasn't sure.

"Whoa there!" Cal sputtered in reply, taking a half-step backward to receive Wendy's momentum, then recovering quickly to embrace and turn her halfway around to face a gray-haired receptionist on the other side of the counter. "This is the daughter," he explained efficiently. "Wendy...?"

Wendy stared distractedly at the woman, then craned her neck to look up at Cal, who somehow explained everything with just a look and a nod of his head. Wendy reached deep into her purse, looking for her wallet, while rapidly announcing the information she thought was needed: "Palmer. My name is Wendy Palmer. My father fell out of a boat and his name is Lucas. My mother is Flora Palmer. She's already dead." Then she gasped and said again, "Oh my God."

"That's all right," Cal murmured soothingly. "That's all right. Goodness, you're white as a sheet. Did you have any trouble getting here? You seem to have made really good time."

"We did," Wendy replied with a fluttery voice, "but Tom..." Words failed her. She turned around again to look helplessly into Cal's warm hazel eyes, not knowing how to explain Tom's behavior.

Cal seemed to pick up a different message. "Your dad's alive, Wendy. He made it here. He's still in Emergency but soon they'll be moving him to Intensive Care."

Wendy gulped. "Is he okay?" she asked, and closed her eyes for the response.

She could feel Cal's deliberate pause. "I won't lie," he said softly. "He's not okay. He's in a coma. If he doesn't come to soon — well, the doctor said it's very serious."

Wendy could think of nothing to say. She realized she was still in Cal's half-embrace and gently shook herself free, resuming the dig in her purse until she got hold of her wallet, which she opened and thrust toward the receptionist. "Here's my driver's license," Wendy announced. "Do you need that?"

Far to her right, from the direction that Wendy had rushed into the building, the sliding glass doors swished open and the efficient background hum of the hospital was abruptly drowned out by a voice imitating a wailing saxophone, followed by a giggle. Tom pranced in wearing his now-incongruous bathing suit and t-shirt, and Cal, obviously taken aback, yelled out "Tom! What the hell are you doing?"

Wendy felt inexplicably guilty and rushed to explain. "I tried to tell you! We had to stop for coffee — just for a minute — and something happened to Tom. He got really weird."

Cal's eyes widened as he reached behind him for a leather pouch that Wendy now noticed was slung over his shoulder. "Tom had *coffee*?" he exclaimed worriedly. "My God, you could have been killed. He's allergic to the caffeine *and* the acids. It's a neurological thing." As Cal drew forth two tea packets from his pouch, his voice grew stern and forbidding: "Dammit, he knows better than that." Then his voice softened: "But I guess he's really scared. Excuse me a minute."

Wendy watched as Cal hurried down the corridor to take Tom into his arms; Tom seemed very happy to see him, and not at all frightened. As they began speaking urgently to each other — too softly for Wendy to hear from fifteen feet away — she felt a cool touch on her forearm and turned her gaze to the receptionist, who was saying, "Miss Palmer, we can take it from here. Do you know about your dad's insurance?"

LUCAS felt as though he were one piece again. His body still had the strange feeling of being lighter than air, but at least he wasn't scattered over the terrain anymore. Now he was sitting beside Flora on a gentle green rise overlooking a sparkling stream about twenty yards downhill. Lucas breathed deeply — the first time he could remember breathing for several hours, it seemed — and felt grateful for the scene he was surveying.

"Flora," he asked calmly, "where are we exactly?"

Flora pushed back her luxuriant red curls with one hand and replied, "You could call this the real world, dear. Everything has been forgiven here."

Lucas didn't know what that meant but he sensed a connection anyway. "Is that why everything is so beautiful?"

"Uh-huh," Flora smiled gaily, leaning forward to grasp both her ankles and rest one cheek on her knees, looking happily at Lucas the same way she had done as a young girl at college, when they fell in love. "But it's just a way-station. You can think of it as a vacation spot, dear, a little resting place before you — go on to the next thing." Flora's face clouded as if she knew something she couldn't confide. Then she added, "You're not supposed to be here yet but everything has gotten out of order, thanks to your friend the General. Some hero you've got there, honey."

"Patton!" Lucas exclaimed, recalling with a shock everything that had transpired in the amphitheater. "He said I was too much of a coward to see the Vision."

"Oh dear," Flora sighed, lying back on the grass. "The Vision. The big picture. The grand universal theory. You men are always so... *menlike*."

This sounded funny to Lucas. "Even here?" he chuckled, looking back at Flora and noticing that she seemed to be growing younger by the second. "Aren't we men forgiven here too?" For a second he felt a strong sexual arousal in his groin, but the energy rapidly shot up his spine and seemed to leap, fountain-like, out the top of his head and condense rapidly in the air above them, resulting in several seconds of a spritzing rain-shower. "What the devil?" sputtered Lucas, raising his hands in wonderment and looking helplessly at Flora.

But she hadn't seemed to notice. Now she was sitting up straight and regarding him with very serious eyes. Lucas could swear she was twenty years younger than a few moments before. She grasped his wrist firmly and said, "Lucas. I can't explain everything that's happened. Let's say you took an accident in order to accelerate certain processes. From here you can help things happen in a way you couldn't before."

"What kind of things?" Lucas asked soberly, moved by his

wife's seriousness.

"Wendy," she replied simply. "Wendy's stuck and we have to help her. We have a channel to her but we have to clear up some things between ourselves to get through to her. Are you ready to work with me, dear?"

"Sure," Lucas concurred. In fact he didn't have the slightest idea of what they were talking about. "What should we do?"

"Oh honey," Flora cried out unexpectedly, her voice markedly higher and charged with panic. When Lucas looked at her again, she had abruptly become the young girl he loved in college, wearing the long hippie skirt and multiple bracelets he hadn't seen on her in decades. She was crying freely and suddenly leapt into his arms, hugging him fiercely around the neck. "I'm just not ready, Luke," she confided in his ear. "I'm too scared. What are we going to do?"

Chapter 6

After filling out forms for the receptionist at the entry desk, Wendy asked to see her father. The motherly volunteer said he was still in the ER. "Dr. Chambers will come to see you just as soon as your dad has been transferred to the ICU," she said pleasantly. "Why don't you take a seat here in the lobby? It shouldn't be much longer." Perhaps because Wendy was staring at her blankly, her eyes red and wet, the woman rose from her seat and reached out to touch Wendy's forearm.

"I'm so sorry, dear. This must be a terrible shock."

Wendy nodded mutely, having no idea of what to do besides stand rooted to the spot she was occupying by the counter. Cal and Tom approached from her right and Wendy felt Cal gently lay a hand atop her shoulder. He had Tom's elbow in his other hand, and began ushering both of them down a hallway. "We're heading to the café for a while," he informed the receptionist, who regarded the trio quizzically as they traveled down the hall. She had no information on the wiry man who had burst into the lobby singing at the top of his lungs. This wouldn't be the first time that a case from the psych clinic had wandered into the main building. But she couldn't figure the connection with the drowning. She pulled on her ear for a moment, then the intercom board in front of her lit up like a Christmas tree. She decided that the tall handsome fellow had things well in hand.

Inside the well-appointed hospital café, an espresso machine was noisily spitting steam as Cal herded his two charges into the room. Cal glanced at the machine and muttered "Only in California!" under his breath before pointing Wendy toward one chair and saying "I'll be right back." Wendy dropped heavily into the plastic seat and wondered why Cal was taking Tom elsewhere, to the opposite corner of the room about twenty feet away, ordering him to sit and then going to the cashier to ask for a cup of hot water. Cup in hand, he returned to Tom and dunked both of the teabags he had produced earlier into the hot water.

Tom was literally bouncing in his chair, grinning like a drunk and pawing at Cal before the bigger man backed away and walked toward Wendy in a sidewise, crablike fashion, keeping his eyes on his companion all the way. When Cal began lowering himself into a seat beside Wendy, Tom popped up like a jack-in-the-box. Cal shook his head, pointed at Tom and broadcast an unequivocal demand — "Stay!" — as if he were speaking to a puppy. Tom sat back down, frowning childishly. Four other people scattered throughout the café stopped their conversations or magazine reading to eyeball the scene.

Wendy didn't know what to say. She tried to look at Cal meaningfully, but he only smiled curtly and asked, "Can I get you anything?"

"Uh, no," Wendy answered. "Not right now." Then she couldn't stand it anymore. She tilted her head toward Tom in the far corner of the restaurant — he was starting to sing again, not so loud this time — and inquired in a whisper, "Is he all right?"

Cal raised his eyebrows and looked a little uncertain for the first time since Wendy had encountered him on the pier. He seemed to be composing himself. "Tom is in an overexcited state," Cal finally stated in a firm tone that would have done justice to a documentary. "He'll get back to normal faster if he's by himself for a little while. Chamomile helps too, sometimes."

"Does he have to take medication?" Wendy felt genuinely concerned.

"Tried all that," Cal responded with a sigh. "Nothing worked like it should. Sedatives don't exactly calm him down, they just make him mopey. Once we tried Xanax for a week and he started planning his funeral. Said he could see the end coming. Listen, how much coffee did he have anyway?"

Wendy glanced nervously across the café, unsure of whether she should tell the whole truth. "Two cups. Three maybe?"

"Decaf," Cal responded sternly, as if his preference could dictate history.

"Um, no," Wendy replied weakly, feeling like a snitch. "He said we needed to make time on the road."

"Oh, man," Cal exclaimed, lowering his blond head to rub it all over with one hand before returning his gaze to Wendy with a wicked smile. "I'll bet you did, too, huh?"

Wendy nodded her head with wide eyes and then leaned forward to whisper. "Something else happened," she confided. "Tom started talking in this little boy's voice. He said that he could see my father, and that he was with my mother somewhere. He knew my mother's name."

Instead of answering, Cal cast a murderous look at his companion, who smiled, waved, and impishly made a zipping motion across his lips. Cal's grim expression instantly broke into a grin and he returned his attention to Wendy with a helpless shake of the head. "Ya gotta love this guy, don't you think?" he laughed.

Wendy was still leaning forward, intently curious. "Cal, is Tom like a psychic or something?"

Cal released a big sigh, as if the cat was out of the bag. "Well, not like most psychics," he said condescendingly.

"What do you mean?"

"You ever seen one of those ads for psychics on TV?" Cal asked.

"Once or twice," Wendy said coolly while thinking: *About a hundred times, but then I do have insomnia.*

Cal didn't catch her deception. "Well, you know how they are then." He pitched his voice high into a series of impressions. "Well, this psychic knew I was pregnant! And that psychic knew I had a brother! And this one knew I was buying a car! Every time I see one of those damn ads I start screaming, *You already know these things, people! Get a life!*"

Wendy tried to laugh, but in fact she felt ashamed. She usually found the psychic infomercials riveting — especially when the testimonials included stories of women winning the lottery, getting a great job, meeting a future husband. It seemed that people who consulted psychics had nice, surprising things like that happen to them pretty often. But she had never considered calling the 900 numbers herself because she wasn't the kind of person who attracted big surprises. At least, not until today. And then it had to be the wrong kind of surprise.

Cal seemed a little miffed that Wendy wasn't appreciating his performance. "Anyway," he said dismissively, "Tom isn't psychic like that. When he gets unstable, sometimes he tunes into things. Somehow he picks up information that people *don't* already know about themselves. And they don't always like to hear it."

"Wow," Wendy said softly, truly impressed. She stole a glance at Tom, now sitting quietly with both elbows on the table, hands supporting his chin, looking bored. She turned slowly back to Cal. "Does that mean he really saw my father somewhere?"

"Oh, I don't know," Cal replied briskly. "As you probably heard, Tom taps into a bunch of utter nonsense too. There's a lot of bandwidth in that pretty little head of his. You know, I've really got to visit the little boy's room. Then I'm going to look for Dr. Chambers — I think he should have checked in with us by now." Cal stood and extended one hand to touch Wendy lightly on the shoulder. "Will you be all right for a few minutes? Maybe you should get yourself something to eat."

Wendy shook her head and said, "No thanks. I mean, thanks for looking for the doctor but I'm okay."

Cal disappeared. Wendy cast her eyes to the food counter but realized that she actually wasn't hungry after all, nor even confused about whether she was hungry — an unusual degree of clarity for her. "Maybe I need more emergencies in my life," she muttered ruefully, then flashed on a memory of Tom hunched over the wheel of the VW, pushing the bug upwards of seventy miles an hour and singing like a madman.

She shifted in her seat to see what Tom was up to now. The far corner of the room was empty. There was a light, tentative tap on her opposite shoulder, and Wendy nearly jumped out of her chair sideways as she turned to find Tom standing very close to her, leaning down into her face with glassy eyes.

The little-boy voice was whispering: "*They couldn't tell you...*" Tom hesitated, blinking rapidly, creasing his brow.

"Couldn't tell me what?" Wendy whispered back, her skin crawling.

"*They couldn't tell you when you were really born.*"

OF ALL the moments from his past Lucas might have wanted to revisit, this was not it: the moment that his youth effectively ended and all the responsibilities, regrets, and half-truths of his adult life took root. Flora was crying on his shoulder just like she did years ago when she revealed the pregnancy, and he felt the same heart-stopping terror that he had known as a junior at Chico State. This was the moment when the chronic unfairness of his life had begun. It seemed doubly unfair that he had to live through it again in his memory.

If he had to go back in time, he vastly preferred the moment from one year earlier, when he first met Flora at the frat house. There he had been with a messy array of notes and topographical maps spread over the enormous dining room table. It was a hot spring, and Lucas had propped open the front door and pushed up the old, warped windows as far as he could to get the most out of infrequent breezes. When one errant zephyr blew through with vigor, it kicked up half his papers and deposited them in swirls and curls all over the foyer of the old house. As he rushed to retrieve them, a voluptuous redhead coed in open-toed sandals, sunglasses and a short skirt — daringly short for 1967 in Chico — strode in through the open front door and bent down to pick up a single sheet.

Always awkward in front of attractive women, Lucas felt especially unprepared to meet this knockout, dressed as he always was in his faded Bermuda shorts and untucked white Arrow shirt, the kind that his mother sent him in batches every few months. He stopped his paper-gathering and just stared open-mouthed at the young woman before him, who seemed to be studying a sheet with his sketch of an ancient volcanic formation in the faraway Hebrides as if it meant something to her. Finally she pulled her sunglasses halfway down the bridge of her nose and remarked coolly, "This shoah looks like fun." Her voice was surprisingly Southern; her smile was bigger and friendlier than Lucas thought he could possibly deserve.

In one of his few times of solidarity with his "brothers," Lucas had spent the night before in a group improvisation of sure-fire lines to use on Chico's finest young females. Fueled from the keg that sat on top of the TV, the exercise had quickly degraded into raunchy vulgarities. But Lucas had almost wanted to take notes on some of their more sober attempts at early-stage seduction. He sure could have used a decent line now, as the young woman's own opener fell awkwardly into the silence of the big open house. Lucas could not recall a single suave rejoinder to use on well-rounded girls who picked up one's notes for Geography 303. He just stood there thinking he was an idiot.

Finally the beautiful girl laughed and extended an elegant hand, tipped with crimson nails, to lay gently on Lucas' right shoulder. "Look heah darlin'," she drawled conspiratorially, "why don't you think up sumthin' to say while I look for Chet Townsend. Can you point in the general direction where I might find him?"

Lucas' heart sank like a stone. If the house's ultimate smooth mover was in this game, he was already on the bench. His only advantage was that neither Chet nor the rest of the guys were in attendance that Saturday morning. On Chet's impulse they had all blasted down to some SoCal beach town for the weekend, leaving Lucas with a coveted thirty-six hours of study time.

It was this kind of studious, anti-social behavior — among other things — that would eventually induce the guys to ask him to find other lodgings.

But for the moment Lucas' unconventional work habits seemed to be his saving grace. When he found his tongue and explained the emptiness of the house to the young woman, she explained in turn that she had merely come to fetch a textbook of hers that Chet had accidentally picked up in a class they shared. "Accidentally my ass!" Lucas blurted without thinking. His sudden expletive induced a burst of raucous laughter from the redhead. Pressing his unexpected advance against Chet, Lucas then shared his speculation that looking in the dorm directory to find the number associated with the name in the textbook — Flora Sanders, as it turned out — was probably the first original research Chet had done in three years of college.

"Oh, stop it now!" Flora had responded with another big laugh and another forward touch, this time on Lucas' chest. Her accent seemed to be growing stronger as his knees felt weaker. But Lucas had to admit a grudging admiration for the house leader: "Convincing you to come over here for your book instead of bringing it to you — now that's pretty smooth."

"Not too smooth," Flora rejoined. "He ain't heah."

"No he ain't," said Lucas in an unintended imitation, feeling pretty smooth himself.

Flora Sanders winked at him and said, "Tell you what. Why don't you write down my phone number and when Chet gets back, you get my book from him and give me a call. Can you do that for me, Mister — uh?"

"Lucas. Just call me Lucas." He couldn't believe he hadn't said his own name before now. He also couldn't believe what had just happened to him, Lucas Palmer, the last guy who would ever come up with a smooth move.

Lucas smiled in recollection of that victorious moment from so long ago, realizing with a start that the young Flora was still sobbing into his shirt. The peculiarity of the situation now dawned fully upon him: Flora was young and he wasn't; they weren't back in Chico but sitting in a too-perfect, gently rolling meadow by a tinkling stream. A picnic basket full of sparkly diamonds lay right beside him. Lucas was about to ask Flora exactly what was going on when she sat up straight, wiped the tears from her eyes with trembling fingers from both hands, and whimpered, "I just don't understand how this happened!"

Lucas had to laugh out loud. Even now, some thirty years later, he could sure as hell remember how it happened. Looking back, the miracle was that it had taken a whole year after their first meeting for it to happen, given their youthful sexual enthusiasm and inadequate precautions. While their first date had started off awkwardly — Lucas had promised Flora a surprise and led her blindfolded into the Geography library to show her the really good topo maps — it had ended quite sensually, with Flora cuddling up next to him in a great little Italian restaurant that she had suggested. Lucas had never heard of it; he had hardly gone out until that point in his college career.

After dinner they had talked and laughed together for hours, until the waiter told them at one a.m. that they had to leave. Outside her dorm, Flora had grabbed onto Lucas and kissed him passionately, complete with thrusting tongue, then flounced into the huge white edifice with a backward wave of her fingers. She left Lucas in a state of sexual intoxication that was novel for being induced by an actual female, close-up.

When he returned to the house, big Chet Townsend was draped over the couch in front of the TV and accosted Lucas as if he were the watchful father of an errant teen. When Lucas happily started into the whole story, beginning with the topo maps, Chet interrupted with a sneer. "Jesus, Palmer, you're such a loser. Why don't you just hand over this little redhead now, before I have to make a move on her and make you feel all sad inside? You might remember that she came to see me in the first place, Filthy Luker."

Everything that Lucas disliked about Chet — his arrogant perch at the top of the house pecking order, the natural athleticism that let him get away with academic laziness, and especially the hateful nickname he had tagged onto Lucas when he found out about the moderate fortune so tightly managed by Lucas' mother — coalesced into one unprecedented surge of unwise rebellion. "Go to hell, Townsend," he seethed, and stomped upstairs to the mansion's stuffy, half-converted attic, his room. He would be looking for his first apartment within two months....

Lucas blinked, trying to get control of the way his mind kept sinking so completely into these collegiate reveries. The young Flora was still sniffling, trying to dry her face, looking up at him with a mixture of fear and utter dependency. He recalled with a shock that this was one of the things he'd long forgotten that had cemented their early relationship — the way Flora genuinely looked up to him from the day they met, despite his social awkwardness, lack of worldliness, and narrow range of interests.

And God, she was beautiful — *is beautiful*, he thought in confusion, reaching out now to gently cradle the young Flora's chin in a way that he had probably never done as a young man. Flora's beauty had simply overwhelmed him back then, like a gift handed down from the Olympians for their own entertainment

— to watch a mere mortal flounder and drown in the midst of beauty meant for the gods. And flounder he did, losing a whole point in his grade average in the first semester after meeting Flora, losing his place to live due to Chet's jealousy, and having to ask his mother for rent money plus increased living expenses.

The latter humiliation owed largely to Flora's penchant for jaunts down to San Francisco to catch pricey opening nights at the American Conservatory Theatre. She had friends in the acting school there, and she glided through packed pre-show lobbies, crowded mezzanines, and anxiety-racked backstages with the ease of a fish through water. For the taciturn Lucas, the whole scene was always a shock — not to mention a crash course in cultural arts.

Of course Flora had also come up with the idea of sleeping over in the City at one fancy hotel after another, never the same one twice. Actually, Lucas recalled with a smirk, there had been precious little sleep taking place on those deliciously illicit field trips — the first compelling reason he had ever found to lie to his mother. The couple took their first trip about a month after they met, following four dates that had ended in progressively heated states of erotic hesitation. By the late sixties the so-called sexual revolution might have been well underway for San Francisco flower-children, but Lucas and Flora were from the hinterlands.

On their Chico dates they were limited to making out in semi-public places — darkened movie theaters, the park downtown as dusk fell, Lucas' funky blue Chevy Nova — because the frat house was not the place to bring a woman into under the best conditions. And ever since Lucas had "stolen" Flora from Chet Townsend, the conditions in the house couldn't have been worse for romance. Chet was waging a cold-war campaign against Lucas' right to exist under the same roof as his fraternity brothers. Flora still lived in a women's dorm where visiting males were shown the door by floor monitors at nine p.m. That's why the young couple would eventually consummate their building sexual tension in a tony hotel room in San Francisco.

In fact, Flora would not have had it any other way. Only later would Lucas comprehend how artfully she had engineered the whole set-up at the Sir Francis Drake. On their first trip to San Francisco they had driven down in the middle of a Friday afternoon — Lucas missing two classes and a significant exam in the process — and sauntered into the big hotel presumably on a lark, Flora idly chattering about how she could act her way into a free room for the weekend if she really felt like it. Lucas was always entertained by his girl's flights of fancy (back in those days, anyway) and he had laughed aloud, "Well, this would be a good time to feel like it. Otherwise we have to drive back to Chico tonight," he said sternly. He pulled out his wallet and pinched it with two fingers, like drafting calipers, to emphasize its thinness.

So Flora, who was dressed to kill in something silky and plum-red, proceeded forthrightly to the reservations desk, discreetly keeping the cheaply attired Lucas directly behind her, out of the line of sight. In her heaviest drawl she announced that she was "Tandy Savannah," the Broadway actress who had just flown in from New York as an emergency understudy for the problematic female lead in that night's premiere of "The Glass Menagerie."

"Mah directuh said the hotel has an arrangement with the thea-tah?" Flora had haughtily dictated to the concierge, who nodded doubtfully and stepped back to dial a phone behind him. Lucas cringed and tugged on Flora's elbow to get her out of there before they were royally shown the door. In a few moments the concierge stepped forward with a bright smile and said "Of course, Miss Savannah. We're so honored to have you with us. That will be the Theater Suite for yourself and...?"

Flora turned and gave Lucas a wink and a dazzling grin, and said simply, "Mah-self and mah young assistant, if you please." That night after the show, there was free champagne in the room, plus a huge flower arrangement with a card that said "Congratulations on your brilliant career Tandy!" Flora spent half an hour in the bathroom before emerging in a sheer, floor-length gown that both veiled and revealed her full-bodied sensuality.

Lucas was so distracted by the heady otherworldliness of their illicit tryst that he couldn't properly remember how to be forceful and manly, and instead spent almost an hour tracing his fingers over Flora's naked curves, hills, and valleys, as if he were surveying a splendid new territory whose every detail should not be missed. Flora moaned and rolled back and forth every now and then, finally pulling Lucas on top of her and directing their joining.

But he didn't like it that way and soon rolled them both over. With her full weight upon him, Lucas began to relax instead of getting more excited, and felt that he could remain in that position all night, perpetuating the delicious sensation of having arrived in a foreign but welcoming land. As he said "ahhh" and began letting himself sink into the bed, Flora thrust down hard on him and laughed: "Hey loverboy, don't y'all go to sleep on me now!"

Lucas smiled fuzzily, eyes closed, and mumbled without meaning to, "Why not Chet Townsend?"

There was such a long silence that Lucas opened his eyes

to see Flora regarding him with a look of tender puzzlement. "He's really getting to you, ain't he?" she said tenderly. Then a big tear rolled from one eye as she lowered herself, her breasts flattening warmly against Lucas, and whispered in his ear. "Oh, you dear gentle man. You don't even know why you've got it all over Chet Townsend, do you? Well, I do. And Lord knows I've had enough of his kind..." She held Lucas tightly, and wept a little more, then slowly slid off his body and cuddled beside him for the night. In the morning they finished what they had begun.

That was the beginning of the sexual good times which, alas, would not last very long. Lucas liked to blame their short duration on the Summer of Love, in which he could rightfully claim that he and Flora were literal participants (since they once did it right in Golden Gate Park that very August). But while Lucas maintained a certain disdain for the whole hippie scene, sticking to his short hair and white shirts against a veritable flood of men's long dirty locks and tie-dyed T's, Flora steadily gravitated toward the flower-child culture in both style and consciousness. She began wearing fewer tight short skirts and more long, flowing ones, and became obsessed with everything "natural" — from food to footwear to, unfortunately, birth control. Although the term wasn't used back then, Lucas knew that 1967, the year he met Flora, was the same year she began drifting toward the New Age.

Of course it was Flora's notion that she could gauge her fertility cycle by an ornate astrological calendar that got them into big trouble — the trouble they were now revisiting in this otherworldly clime. It was dawning on Lucas that there was something he should say or do for the young terrified girl beside him now, something that he hadn't done when he was equally young and consumed with anxiety. But what? He couldn't change the past, could he? He couldn't change the way it had all gone down after Flora had discovered her pregnancy — especially the way Lucas' mother had taken over their lives.

They went to his mother because Flora's family couldn't possibly have helped. She had never known her real father and mother, and had been raised by her holy-rolling aunt and uncle who would have lapsed into a prolonged snake-handling fit if the news were ever leaked to them — and then gladly condemned Flora as a harlot fit for hell. She had gotten herself out of Alabama courtesy of another, more liberal uncle in Mobile who had money and sent her regular if parsimonious checks out of pity. But an unwed pregnancy wouldn't have gone over too well with the uncle either.

So Lucas had fearfully phoned his mother Agnes at her office in Chicago, acutely aware that his predicament wasn't going to appeal her to habitual if pro forma Catholicism. Add in that all his mother knew about Flora was that she was "a nice girl" he'd taken out to lunch a couple times, and the situation looked especially dicey. So he got the whole confession over with rapidly, spilling the beans in one long breathless rush ending with, "I'm really sorry, Mother, to have to ask for your help this way. I know this isn't right, and not according to my academic plan."

There had been a long silence after which Agnes spoke in the tone she always reserved for the business of her late husband's estate — clear, decisive, and to Lucas' ears at this moment, shatteringly final. "I'll arrange a civil ceremony next month here in Chicago where no one knows us. Flora can move into the house in Sacramento for a while. I was planning to rent it anyway; I just can't go back there. You'll continue in school until you finish next year. We can make this look all right, Luke, but there's one thing you must promise me without fail."

"Yes, Mother?" he had replied weakly, his head spinning, his heart strangely aching for some sign of personal displeasure from his mother.

"The child must never know," Agnes dictated. "We'll get the birth certificate fixed; that shouldn't be too difficult. You'll just have to celebrate her first birthday twice, I guess. At least she'll have a little edge on the other kids when she reaches school age. Do you understand me, son?"

Lucas had seen his mother take control of emergencies before — like his dad's horrific heart attack when he was twelve — but he had never heard her like this. How could she have already thought this far ahead? he wondered. And how did she know the baby would be female?

There was no way she could have known, of course. Yet everything unfolded just as she dictated on that fateful day in February of 1968. Flora quit school in Chico and moved to Sacramento, which pleased her at first because she had a sizeable house — the house in which Lucas had spent the latter half of his childhood — and she was that much closer to her dramatic pals in San Francisco. Lucas stayed in school but spent every weekend in Sacramento until Wendy's birth late in '68. Once her birth certificate was fixed to say 1969, all the rescheduling of the infant's life was built upon that single document. Lucas and Flora did indeed celebrate Wendy's first birthday again when she was two.

When she was a toddler people would sometimes say "My, she's big for her age!" but the fact that Wendy was always big helped cover the deception. When she entered grade school, it turned out that she needed all the advantage she could get to stay even with her peers. Her father couldn't court the notion that his daughter was anything less than bright; he would always write off her problems in school to the fact that Wendy had been emotionally unstable since age two (well, three). In fact she had seen her first therapist at four (five).

But Wendy's instability wasn't the problem that faced Lucas now. Flora was still crying and shivering against him. Since he was now fifty and she was still twenty, it was undoubtedly his responsibility to set things right. But how? If he couldn't literally alter their history, what could he do for Flora now that would make any difference? He thought back to the terribly awkward period of Flora's difficult pregnancy, how the joy and playfulness of their early relationship had so abruptly disappeared and been replaced with her daily nausea and his grim sense of duty. He remembered the shameful feeling of being little more than an intermediary between his new wife and his mother, whose purse strings would be entangled with every decision or move he made until he finished graduate school when Wendy was five (six).

And then, with a shocking twist of pain in his heart, Lucas recalled one of the many awful arguments with Flora during the pregnancy when she had shouted, "I don't care about your mother's damn money! I just wish you were really here with me! You're not ever *with* me anymore!" and he had coolly replied, "I come here every damn weekend to be with you," and then stalked out of the Sacramento house to take a long, lonely, self-righteous walk by the river.

So that was it. Now that he knew what he must do, the awareness seemed so simple. Yet it had taken him thirty years, an incomprehensible calamity, and removal to this strange realm for him to grasp such a little thing. Gently he pulled

Flora away from his tear-wetted chest and smiled into her red-rimmed eyes. "Flora?" he whispered softly.

"Uh-huh?" she mumbled, as precious as a child.

"You're my girl," he said firmly. "I'll be right here with you all the way."

Flora gasped, smiled, and said "Really?" and gave him a crushing hug. When she sat back a few moments later, Lucas watched with amazement as her face began to age, the tiniest wrinkles beginning to show at the corners of her eyes, her cheeks and neck filling out perceptibly with the weight she had gained later. Lucas sensed that they were moving on. Did this mean they would now revisit some other time from their life together? Was that what Flora had meant earlier when she said they had to clear up some things between them before they could help Wendy, who was "stuck" somewhere?

Lucas looked to Flora's changing visage for further clues. He could tell that she was about to speak his name when she cocked her head strangely, frowning toward the green hillock behind his left shoulder. Lucas turned to face the same direction. Then he could hear the noise. Unless he was mistaken, the grind-and-clank, grind-and-clank clatter emanating from behind the hill in this strange paradise belonged to a rapidly approaching Sherman tank.

Chapter 7

"SIT DOWN! Sit down!" Wendy urged Tom, halfway embarrassed that they might be on the way to making a scene in the hospital café, and halfway anxious not to lose contact with the knowing child who was speaking through Tom again. Tom slipped into the seat beside Wendy, his eyes bright with excitement. Wendy reached out to clasp Tom's forearm and pull him a little closer. She cast her eyes from side to side like an amateur spy and said quietly, "What do you mean, they couldn't tell me when I was really born?"

Tom tittered like a boy who's just told a silly joke, breaking from Wendy's touch to clap his hands together. "You had your number one birthday two times!" he laughed in delight. He began bouncing in the seat and Wendy reached out again to grab him, this time exerting a little force to keep him in place. "The same party!" Tom giggled. "The same party!"

Something clicked in Wendy's head but she couldn't put a finger on it. She began searching Tom's face for a sign that he was putting on an act, although for the life of her she couldn't imagine why he would, especially just for her. A clear sign of fakery would at least mean she could dismiss everything Tom's child voice said from now on. Not only was the whole thing spooky; Wendy had the nagging sensation that she might soon hear things she'd really rather not. That's what Cal had warned, after all. She decided to give Tom a test, affecting a schoolteacher's diction to phrase it:

"Now Tom, why would my folks give me the same birthday party twice? That's not a normal thing to do."

Tom cocked his head, looking puzzled for a moment, and then grinned at Wendy as if she were the dumbest girl on the playground. "Grammuh Aggie told 'em to," he insisted.

Even with all her weight on the seat, Wendy pushed backward so violently that the legs of the chair made a loud *skraacking* noise on the floor, drawing everyone's attention to her. She took a deep breath and intoned "This is too much," before noticing that Tom's childlike energy was dissipating. The corners of his eyes dropped; his skin wrinkled slightly before her very eyes, and the little boy was gone.

"Man, I'm wasted," Tom said in his normal voice, scanning the room in all directions before locking eyes again with Wendy. "So where's Cal?"

Before Wendy could put together a coherent answer, Tom shrugged his shoulders and lay his head down on top of his folded arms on the table. Almost immediately he fell into a rhythmic, sleeping pattern of breath. After a few moments Wendy reached out tentatively to pat his head, saying "Tom?" faintly, although her mind was somewhere else. She was trying to remember her childhood birthday parties one by one, even though she knew the first would be beyond her ken, and probably the second. Although she couldn't come up with any specific memories of cakes or balloons, she did keep seeing Gramma Aggie's stern, patrician face before her, smiling that painful smile that always made Wendy feel like she was some kind of vexation.

Deep inside, well beneath the level of conscious thought and memory, Wendy sensed something that had always been crazily fluttering within her begin to steady itself — as if a wildly unstable gyroscope lodged in her solar plexus had been subtly tipped toward its center of gravity, and began spinning closer to true. "Hmph," Wendy muttered thoughtfully, sitting back in her seat. "The same party..."

She would be sitting in the same position ten minutes later, her glazed eyes staring at the far wall of the hospital café, when Cal appeared in the entryway. He was followed by a huge black man wearing huge black-framed eyeglasses and a doctor's white coat. Cal came abreast of Wendy and pointed to the sleeping Tom, remarking matter-of-factly, "It was the Kid, wasn't it?"

"Hunh?" Wendy said, disoriented by her reverie. "What kid?"

"Tom must have been talking in the Kid's voice again," Cal said, stepping around Wendy to tousle Tom's black hair. "That's the really spooky one. He's usually dead-on when the Kid comes through, but it tires him out. He always falls asleep like this — like it's naptime in kindergarten."

"Excuse me," boomed the black doctor, "what are we talking about? Is this Mr. Palmer's daughter? I'm on a short leash today, as I told you already."

Cal whipped around angrily to face the physician, started to say something but then apparently thought better of it and turned instead to give Wendy a rolling-eyes look of exasperation. She couldn't quite get his drift, and her eyes were drawn to the bigger man anyway. He was as black as Yaphet Kotto, Wendy's favorite actor on "Homicide," a TV show that she'd taken to watching lately. The doctor was younger than Kotto, thirty at most. And he was enormous — not as fat as Wendy felt, but both tall and wide, seeming to fill up the drab café with more than his physical presence. Wendy was awestruck.

One of her secrets was that she found large black men mysteriously exciting. They seemed to own a magical tribal potency that had less to do with sexuality than natural authority: the ability to make dramatic decisions and carry lesser mortals along in their wake, the way Kotto's police lieutenant carried his detectives, or the way James Earl Jones could sweep you away with just his voice. Wendy had told this particular secret to one therapist, who had pointed out that such men might be seen as the polar opposite of her slight, thin, pale-white and always-compromising father. Wendy felt sure there was more to it than that.

For she had another secret she couldn't even tell the most trustworthy counselor. Every time Wendy thought about big, black, powerful men, she was pretty sure she was reincarnated from some kind of African queen. Her mother used to talk about her life as Cleopatra, after all. To Wendy there was a plausible connection: she and her mom had ancient roots in more or less the same neighborhood.

Wendy stood and snapped to, straightening her posture, gluing her eyes to the nameplate "Dr. H. Chambers" on the physician's robust chest. She couldn't quite bring herself to look into his thick-lensed eyes. "Yes, I'm Wendy Palmer," she said dutifully.

Dr. Chambers brought a clipboard up to rest on his stomach and seemed almost to be reading lines from it. "Sorry about your father, Miz Palmer. As the attending physician I have to tell you he's in a very serious way. Besides the oxygen loss due to his submersion in the water, it appears that he may have suffered a concussion. Do you have any idea how that happened?"

Wendy immediately saw the bright red smear on the side of the rowboat as her father had tumbled into the river. "I think he hit his head on the side of the boat when he fell in, sir."

The doctor pulled down his glasses with one hand and peered at Wendy over the chunky frame, narrowing his eyes. "Dr. Chambers is fine with me, Miz Palmer." He scribbled something on his clipboard and added, "Well, that explains that," and then fell silent, looking back and forth from Cal to Wendy as if he expected a cue.

An awkward moment passed before Cal spoke up, obviously still miffed. "Well Doctor, we would certainly appreciate your suggestion as to what we should do? Is Wendy's dad going to need...?" and then Cal trailed off, looking worriedly back at Wendy.

"I wouldn't go far for the next twenty-four hours," Chambers said in a stentorian tone. "Mr. Palmer is in a comatose condition presently. If he's going to make it we'll know by this time tomorrow. If he isn't, we'll know that too. You can visit him in the ICU this evening, but don't expect it to be much of a visit."

"Doctor!" Cal exclaimed. "Could we have a little sensitivity here? This is the man's daughter and she's had a pretty terrible afternoon."

Chambers took a turning step to face Cal head-on, their eyes meeting at the same level, their intensity equal. "I am not a counselor, Mister, uh —"

"Davidson," Cal replied.

"**MISTER** Davidson," Chambers continued, commencing a strange pattern of speech in which certain syllables were launched from his mouth with an explosive vigor. "The **HOS**-pital has a crisis therapist **ON**-staff if anyone has **NEED** for some **BED**side manner. I have been **TOLD** before that I am not very good at **HAND**-holding so I do not even at**TEMPT** it anymore." He turned toward Wendy and softened his tone a little. "If it's any consolation, you can rest as**SURED** that I will provide your father with sur**PASS**ing care in this critical situation. There's no **MEN**tion of it in the visitors' brochure, but I am the **BEST** doctor."

Cal stepped away from Chambers, rubbing his head all over with one hand, grimacing bitterly. Without meaning to, Wendy rose up on the balls of her feet and asked innocently, "In the whole hospital?" Chambers replied only with a puff of his cheeks and a curt hunch of his shoulders, then turned and walked off. Wendy came back down on her heels.

"No lack of confidence there," Tom commented through a huge yawn, drawing surprised looks from both Cal and Wendy. He sounded perfectly normal, sitting up at the table with his chin resting on one palm.

"What an **ASS**hole," Cal mocked in a seething tone. "I'm sorry about this, Wendy. I don't know if there's anything we can do about changing doctors. I suppose I could complain to...."

"No, don't!" Wendy exclaimed, reaching out to Cal's forearm as if to restrain him physically. "I mean, he's probably really busy and overworked. You know what it gets like around here."

Cal blinked and looked confused. Wendy added in an embarrassed tone, "I mean, if it's anything like on 'ER.'"

Cal looked even more confused and Tom chuckled in response. "It's a TV show, Cal. Popular culture. You should try it sometime. It's poison, of course, but so slow-acting that you hardly notice the effects until it's too late."

To Wendy's surprise, Cal stuck his tongue out at his partner before resuming a businesslike demeanor. "So it looks like we're all going to have to stay in Santa Rosa for tonight, at least," he said briskly. "I think we should get a couple rooms somewhere, and you two can rest up while I drive back to Guerneville and pick up any stuff we need. Wendy, I guess you and your dad were staying at the Townsends' cabin next to us?"

Wendy nodded dumbly, awed once again by Cal's presence of mind. She wondered if she should say something to acknowledge all the time Cal and Tom were giving her freely, but the right words wouldn't come. She didn't mean to be ungrateful. But what if she reminded them of their own lives, and they left her all alone?

"Do you have a key? Did you leave the place unlocked?" Cal inquired.

"Yes, probably," Wendy replied, recollecting herself. "I mean, I should have a key in my purse, but we left the back door open when we went down to the river." Wendy could suddenly see hooded thieves ransacking the Townsends' luxurious resort cabin. "Oh no, we should have locked up before we took off!"

"Nah, don't worry about it," Cal reassured her. "It's pretty quiet around there. I'll lock up when I leave. Should be okay. Do you have some, uh, particular clothes you'd like me to pick up, Wendy?"

Wendy glanced down at herself and her standard uniform, semi-consciously devised years ago for the ease of daily repetition: black, flat-heeled, Chinese slip-on sandals with no socks; black pants of some synthetic stretch fabric that she couldn't name but always got at Ross, just like the commercials said; and an untucked men's white Arrow shirt, taken from her father's archive, provided for him by Gramma Aggie. Cal was now looking at her with a slight distaste, and she felt her face flush. "I guess you could get me another shirt? There's a bunch of 'em with my dad's stuff."

"Hmm," Cal said neutrally. "Underwear?"

"No!" Wendy blurted, really blushing now. "I mean, I'll be okay til tomorrow."

Cal and Tom exchanged meaningful glances. "Well, I'll see what I can dig up for all of us," Cal said conclusively. "If your dad's all right in the morning, maybe we can hit the local department store and do a little shopping."

Within the hour Wendy found herself sitting in a chair by the window of a fourth-floor room at a Days Inn near downtown Santa Rosa. She felt as if she had finally come to a stop after being swept away by the rushing river of the afternoon's events. It was a little after four; she dimly remembered thinking about lunch when she was on the pier, so a scant three or four hours must have passed. It felt like a lifetime.

Cal was on the way back to Guerneville in his classy VW, Tom was presumably napping in the room next door. Cal had found the rooms, insisted on holding them with his credit card, called the hospital and exchanged phone numbers with the ICU nurses' station — Cal had taken care of everything. Wendy was left feeling almost uninvolved save for her relationship to a nearly-drowned man, her father, sleeping close to death back at Memorial Hospital. She stared down at the sun-baked parking lot in front of the hotel as if it were the Sahara — the hot, flat, directionless expanse of her unknown future.

Chapter 8

LUCAS and Flora watched in silence as the metallic roar of an unseen machine gradually materialized from behind the grassy rise they were both watching. Just as Lucas had suspected, the machine was a camouflage-mottled tank of World War II vintage. The reptilian vehicle lunged over the hill and abruptly came to a stop with its turret pointed with deadly accuracy at the married couple. An almost comical squeaking noise emanated from the tank as its turret jerkily rotated a few degrees to the right.

Lucas glanced at Flora to see what she was making of the situation, and recognized that she was now in her early thirties. She was heavier now than a few moments ago but still beautiful, dressed in the blue jeans and Shakespeare sweatshirt she had habitually worn while directing high school plays in the late 70s and 80s. She was squinting at the tank with the same critical gaze she had locked upon young pimply actors when they gave a dubious reading of their lines.

Transfixed by Flora's transformation, Lucas was caught short by the loud cough of an explosion. He turned his head to see a puff of blue smoke rise from the open mouth of the tank turret.

At the same moment something shrieked meanly over his head. He whipped around to see a lovely old oak tree about thirty yards behind him split right down the middle of its trunk, a brief burst of flame and a spray of pulverized wood pulp issuing from the hit. The world he was in shook and blurred.

"Shit!" Lucas cried and leapt to his feet, his eyes casting wildly about for cover. He reached out to pull Flora to safety somewhere, but she refused his hand and slowly rose with a look of disgust on her face.

"I *cannot* work like this," she said petulantly, leaning down to pick up the basket in which she had recollected the sparkling fragments of Lucas' mind, which by now felt whole within him again. "I'm taking these," Flora said with a nod toward the diamonds, "so they don't fall into the wrong hands. When you have finished your business with this... *character*," she sneered, raising her chin toward the tank whose turret was squeaking again, "we'll continue. And Lucas," she added in a motherly tone, as if she were upbraiding an errant boy at play, "please don't take too long? We don't have forever. Not yet, anyway."

"Flora?" Lucas whined helplessly, but she was already striding away, shaking her head and waving backward with her free hand, the other holding firm to the handle of the picnic basket. She seemed to be walking in triple-time, disappearing into a distant wooded valley in just a matter of seconds. Lucas turned back helplessly to look at the tank, saw another puff of smoke, heard another shell scream overhead and watched in wondrous shock as it took out a ragged segment of the very sky — puffy white clouds and perfect blueness disappearing into a deep black void that twinkled with tiny silver stars.

Again and again the turret squeaked, the tank rocked on its tracks, and shell after shell shattered the landscape or the broad arc of sky above. Soon Lucas was left only with shattered remnants of the bucolic natural scene that had seemed whole and solid not long before. It was as if Lucas were standing inside a Christmas ornament that had been shot to pieces from within. Everywhere that the shell of natural sunlight and verdant landscape had been blown away, there was a view to a black and coldly infinite universe.

The tank finally fell silent and a metal cap on its top popped up and fell over, clanking. A helmeted figure hoisted itself from within, swung his legs over the side, and jumped onto a floe of thin earth surrounding the war machine. The soldier flung his helmet to the ground, revealing a sweaty bald head.

"Ah-ha!" Patton shouted, gesturing grandly toward Lucas, waving him to come on down the fragmented hillside. "How's that for your fuckin' *real world*, eh sonny?!" Patton guffawed. Lucas gingerly hopped and stepped toward the general, nervously eyeing the sheer drop-offs into space that bordered every island of earth. He wondered anxiously how long the pieces could stay in place. When he came abreast of Patton a few moments later, the big man roughly embraced him around the shoulders and took a long, loud sniff in through his nose.

"Smell that, son?" All Lucas could smell was the faint aroma of oil and gasoline from the tank; all the smoke and dust from the exploded shells had apparently been sucked into space. "Ah, the stink of battle," Patton declaimed. "Don't you just love it?"

Lucas stared in disbelief at the warrior, now dressed in battle fatigues but still wearing his pearl-handled revolvers. With a chill he recalled how Patton had stuck one of those guns in his mouth and blown his mind apart not long ago. Lucas stepped backward and looked longingly in the direction that Flora had disappeared, realizing that he had no idea of her whereabouts.

"Excuse me, sir," he ventured, "but I really need to look for my wife. We were in the middle of something important."

Patton reached out and grabbed Lucas by his upper arm, pulling him close for a whispered intimacy. "Listen to me, son. You don't need to go through all that touchy-feely horseshit. That's not a man's way to the Vision."

"The Vision, sir?" Lucas responded weakly, hearing himself repeat words he immediately regretted. "I'm not sure I understand."

Patton made no violent moves this time, instead stepping away to join his hands behind his back, jutting his chin into the air to survey the strange, piecemeal realm they stood in. "Sure you do, son. Think hard. The Vision — the big picture, the grand universal theory."

"Oh," Lucas responded, nodding his head without comprehension, afraid to express any more doubt or ignorance.

"I've been trying to figure the right angle of attack," Patton continued as he turned and walked to the rear of the tank. He reached into his pocket for a ring of keys, and then opened a panel that glinted brightly in the sun; it looked remarkably like the trunk lid on Lucas' silver 1979 Mercedes. From inside the tank Patton hefted a folding card table that Lucas recognized as the same one which sat on the sunporch of the Sacramento house for years — where he, Flora, and Wendy had played so many weekend rounds of cards when Wendy was still a child. Those were not bad times, Lucas recalled with a nostalgic twinge.

Patton pulled out the table's legs, set it roughly on the ground beside the tank, then returned to the open compartment and pulled forth a canvas sack with the stenciled lettering **THIRD ARMY COMMAND DISPATCH**. Patton up-ended the sack and out of its mouth fell a messy array of maps — topo maps, highway maps, maps tucked inside Wendy's National Geographics, guide maps to tourist destinations like Yellowstone and Yosemite, and city maps. With a start Lucas realized that they were all the maps he had ever owned from his college days forward. The last one to drop out of the sack was one of northern California, on which Lucas had carefully outlined his last trip from Sacramento to Guerneville. Seeing it again made him feel queasy.

Patton was leaning over the table rummaging through the maps like a madman, unfolding some, pushing others off the table, muttering under his breath about "superior forces" and "lines of sight" and "strategic disadvantage." Lucas was increasingly certain that they were wasting valuable time, and he no longer felt much threat from the General. "I'm sorry, sir, but you're going to have to brief me on this," he asserted. "I have no idea of this big vision that you're talking about."

Patton straightened up and regarded him with a wry smile. "You don't, eh? Well then, we've got one helluva peculiar situation on our hands."

"We do?" Lucas queried.

"Damn right we do," Patton growled, reaching deep into the pile of papers on the table to bring forth an inch-thick ring-binder notebook that had so far escaped Lucas' attention. "Because the Vision is not my big idea, sonny — it's yours."

He thrust the notebook at Lucas' face. On the cover was a typed label that said
THE GEOGRAPHIC WHOLE:
Proposal for a Dissertation on the Implicit Dimensions of a Full Earth Survey
by Lucas Palmer, BS

"Oh my God," Lucas whispered, feeling a wave of long-forgotten woe overtake him. He was doubly upset to experience any feelings related to the proposal Patton had produced, a proposal that Lucas distinctly remembered burning in the back yard in Sacramento. He had long ago convinced himself that all emotions associated with the utter defeat of his big idea had burned up along with the paper and cheap plastic binding.

But if his bitter feelings about "The Geographic Whole" were returning in force, the ideas behind the paper were not. Slowly reaching out to take the binder from the grinning General, Lucas felt apprehensive about seeing his sophomoric writing again. He needn't have worried. By the time he began flipping through the pages, cradling the notebook in both arms, his eyes were so full of tears that he couldn't focus on a single word. Or perhaps the words themselves were unfocused; he could have sworn that they were in motion, swirling like rivers of smoke. At any rate the pages were impossible to read. He shut the notebook and held it tight against him; suddenly he felt transported to the last time he had held it so closely and tearfully.

He had just left the office of his doctoral advisor, Dr. Royal Martin, after the secret dream of his college years had been shot down in flames. To say that his day had been ruined would have been a colossal understatement. At that moment the 24-year-old Lucas felt certain that the ruination of his life was complete — a ruination that had begun with the unexpected pregnancy, a rushed marriage, and the premature burden of family obligations. But those were shocks that Lucas could abide. Life was unpredictable, after all, and he still loved Flora, even if their original passion was now more guarded, episodic, hemmed in by adult restrictions and responsibilities. They had not been to a show or a swank hotel in San Francisco, for instance, since Wendy's birth.

Still, that much unfairness Lucas could live with. The rejection of his doctorate proposal was simply too much. It wasn't just the defeat of his ideas that rankled him, but the fact that Royal Martin had vanquished him. Lucas would have to finish his academic career under the total domination of the unctuous, oily-headed son of a bitch, mainly because that was the only way to guarantee himself a similarly safe university career — which was now about the best he could expect from life.

His subjugation would have surprised none of Lucas' graduate peers in Davis, who had always regarded Lucas as a lapdog to Prof. Martin. A consummate university player, Martin had retained his post at the head of the Geography Department for a dozen years primarily through his touch for campus politics rather than any distinction earned in his field. Lucas had found it quite natural, at first, to fall under the sway of the most conservative instructor in the Earth Sciences during the period of the early 70s. Political and cultural upheavals were disturbing college campuses worldwide, even in the agricultural flatlands of Davis. But Lucas wanted no part of social protests, rock music, or drugs. He had always known he was just smart enough to excel only with determined and perpetual study, and his mother expected no less of him. Besides, Flora was enough of a liberal free-thinker for both of them.

Yet the young Lucas felt deeply that that there was more to him than his peers and professors could detect. His cautious, conservative streak was balanced — or so he liked to think until that awful moment outside Royal Martin's office — by a vein of visionary genius. He had poured all that genius into one secret, noble concept that he called "The Geographic Whole."

The idea had first begun to form when he was an undergraduate; he would find himself making odd, unwarranted notes about it between classes and after exams — any time the usual pressure lifted and his mind could wander beyond immediate objectives. He had been making some notes on the big idea the morning he met Flora, as a matter of fact, although he would not tell her about it until after they were married, and then only tentatively. For until he began to write it up as a grad student, he was not sure of its genius.

But as Lucas became sure of it, he also became certain that "The Geographic Whole" would be his ticket out of a humdrum career track as a geography professor, and onto the gravy train of research grants, corporate underwriting, expense-paid world travel, and — well, why not? — world fame as the first mild-mannered geography grad student ever to write a dissertation that became a best-selling nonfiction title. In fact the word 'Pulitzer' had cropped up amongst his penciled notes for "The Geographic Whole" more than once, although he was always sure to erase it thoroughly. If the notes themselves were ever published, he didn't want to look like an arrogant (though prescient) genius.

The sweetest part of it all was that "The Geographic Whole" would serve as a devastating comeuppance to Dr. Martin, who had slowly but surely earned Lucas' enmity the longer he toiled in the old man's shadow. Sure he was a lapdog; it didn't feel good to lose what few friends he had in the department by kowtowing to Martin's every directive for two and a half years. But if any of them knew what was coming, Lucas used to tell himself, they'd have wanted to stay close just to pick up a little of his wake after publication of "The Geographic Whole"...

All of which lay in tatters as Lucas held onto himself and

his binder, trying not to fly apart inside, after Martin had reamed him out over the proposal. He had turned it in two weeks earlier, and was agreeably surprised when Martin had slipped a note in his mailbox at the teaching assistants' lounge, saying "Palmer — my office, 3pm Friday. About your proposal. Urgent." The old man was in shock, for sure, and wanted to pull Lucas immediately out of his TA position (as Lucas had suggested in his cover letter) and get him to work on his dissertation full-time. The "urgent" part was probably about Lucas' additional suggestion that Martin go to bat for him to procure a grant for the globe-girdling survey trip necessitated by his ambitious proposal.

Lucas had floated into the office on clouds of anticipation. He had to admit to himself that he was looking forward to seeing a little humility on Martin's face for the first time ever; the old man would surely have to admit that he'd been bested by a lowly grad student. And the first few words out of Martin's mouth fit the bill.

"I have to say, Palmer, that this —" Martin gestured to the ring-binder between them on the professor's desk — "is one of the most astonishing things I have ever seen as a professor and graduate advisor." Lucas nodded and smiled. "It is utterly..." Martin paused, raking a couple of long oily strands of hair over his shiny pate while seeming to struggle for the right word, "*vacuous*. I told you that I was not comfortable with you spending so much time on this proposal without letting me see any first drafts or portions in progress. Now I see that you've squandered precious months of time — time you can ill afford this late in your graduate career."

"Sir?" was all Lucas could get out, his head spinning only slightly faster than his gut, his hands beginning to clench the arms of his chair.

Martin picked up the notebook and began flipping through it with disdain, leaning back in his squeaky chair. "I never took you for a hippie, Palmer," the professor sighed. "I would still find it hard to believe that you are a drug addict. But how else could you possibly come up with this utter nonsense?" He began reading Lucas' synopsis titles aloud: "Round the World in 80 Ways ... A View from the Top ... Seeing the Whole in the Fragments ... Toward a Meta-Geography ... *Toward a meta-geography*, Palmer? What the hell is that supposed to mean? This is not a good time to switch your career track to philosophy, young man." He slapped the binder back down on the table, hard, and sat forward in his chair, pointing at Lucas, who had no blood remaining in his face.

"I don't even want an explanation of how this all came to pass," Martin continued. "Because there can't be a sensible explanation for this. Palmer, my boy, I didn't take you under my wing to see you crash and burn. This isn't just your reputation at stake. Whatever personal problems you're dealing with, the drugs or whatever, you get them straightened out. And you get your ass back in here Monday morning to talk about what we can do to salvage your academic career. As you know, there were a few stones left unturned in my last paper; maybe we can dig up one of them and polish it in time for you to put together something presentable to the full committee by next year. But mark my words, Palmer — you have wasted precious time on this unintelligible garbage, and my faith in you is sorely tested, young man. Sorely tested."

Still holding the notebook against his chest, Lucas blinked through hot tears and saw Patton looking at him expectantly, a wild-eyed grin dimpling his weathered cheeks. "Well, son," he asked, "you remember now, don't you? So what're you gonna do about this big Vision of yours?"

Lucas looked at Patton blankly, bringing himself back to the present. Then a slow, wicked smile spread across his own face. "You and Flora, you both passed away a while ago, isn't that right, sir?"

Patton nodded enthusiastically. "That's right, sonny. What are you driving at?"

"That means I can look up anybody here," Lucas responded, gesturing in a broad arc at the crazy-quilt scene of pastoral meadow and deep space surrounding them. "That means I can look up Dr. Royal James Martin, God rest his sorry ass."

"Martin, Martin..." Patton muttered, rubbing his chin. "Don't believe I know the man. You say he's a medic? Well, by God we'll find him somewhere in this man's army, if you want him found."

"That's great!" Lucas beamed. "I mean, thank you, sir. And may I ask one other thing?"

"Shoot, son."

Lucas stepped around Patton to approach the tank and rested his proposal for "The Geographic Whole" on top of one its tracks, rattling slightly with the idling engine.

"General Patton, sir," he said with pride, drawing himself up to his full height to cut a proper salute, "I would be honored if you could show me how to work this magnificent machine."

Chapter 9

AFTER a while the low rumble of the air conditioner lulled Wendy to sleep in the hotel room's upholstered chair, where she had been awaiting Cal's return from Guerneville. Leaning slightly to her left with her mouth open, she was dreaming of playing gin rummy with her parents and the effeminate Pierre Townsend, the boy one year younger than herself who was supposed to have been her childhood friend, but instead became something like her mother's son.

Wendy always loved the Saturday afternoon card games; they were some of the rare occasions when her father would come out of his professorial shell, becoming both funny and competitive. Wendy's mother would respond by becoming openly flirtatious, doing things to Dad with her feet under the table and saying racy things that the two kids couldn't really understand but found titillating nonetheless.

Troubled and often weepy by age nine, Wendy would find reasons to giggle through most of these afternoons, the nagging, increasingly persistent question of how she ended up with her parents fading for a little while. "Gin! Gin! I got it!" Wendy barked gaily, and sat straight up with her eyes wide open for a moment, dimly registering the empty hotel room. Then she leaned to her right and fell asleep again.

About thirty-five miles away in Guerneville, Cal was hurriedly wiping clean the kitchen counter of his rented house, muttering under his breath about Tom's incomprehensible capacity to create — and then tolerate — a chaotic mess like the one he had just eliminated. At breakfast that morning Tom had cited his usual defense: "Popovers like this just don't *happen*, darling," and of course he was right. After eating four of them along with a fatty egg breakfast — two indulgences he would never allow himself under any circumstances except vacation — Cal had taken a three-mile run into town and back just so he could get on with the day with both his conscience and his arteries clear.

Then the two of them had read the paper for a while, lounging luxuriously on the back porch before Tom packed up a premature lunch, which they hardly touched before snuggling together on the shore of the river. Tom had said he wanted to talk again (didn't he always?), but as often happened on these trips, talk had gotten waylaid by fooling around. And then, the big woman on the pier, the one who had been sneaking stares at them for twenty minutes, had screamed.

Cal shook his head and hung the damp dishtowel over the oven handle, reflecting with amazement at how quickly one's focus could be changed by accidental events. He was worried about Wendy. She did not look like a person who had taken care of herself up til now, and her prognosis didn't look good if the man Cal had tried to save didn't make it. Cal had the feeling there were not many, if any, other people in her life close enough to care. He glanced at his watch; it was already 5:25 and he hadn't yet been to the Townsends' cabin to get Wendy's things. He looked at the living room — less than perfectly ordered — sighed, and strode to the door, picking up his and Tom's duffel bags and flicking on the exterior flood light before locking up.

As Wendy had suggested, the rear sliding door to the Townsends' place was unlatched. He found himself entering one corner of a spacious den furnished with expensive yet tasteless contemporanea, as if the owner had simply appropriated all the display merchandise at a Sharper Image store. A black leather reclining massage chair sat in another corner facing the enormous television across the way; a matte-black treadmill took up the last corner of the room. On the walls hung a blinding array of polished chrome hubcaps from every luxury car Cal had ever heard of, plus a few more. Oddly, a full-size French flag dominated the wall across from the fireplace, its effect duplicated by the large mirror facing it.

Cal nearly jumped out of his skin when a digital female voice suddenly intoned, "Good evening. It is five-thirty p.m." The voice seemed to have issued from an enormous sheet of plexiglass, easily six feet tall by three wide, standing in a wooden base next to the massage chair. Cal couldn't believe that it had so far escaped his notice. When he approached it, perplexed, he could see that within the clear pane of plastic was fixed a hologram of an old grandfather clock. A small speaker was embedded in the base of the strange appliance.

"Holy hell," Cal laughed aloud, "there oughta be a law." He started for the entry to a nearby hallway when his eye was caught by a silver-framed photograph on the fireplace mantel. When he peered at it closely, he saw an assembly of six strangers, a few of whom began to look familiar the longer he stared.

Across the picture's width was a gleaming silver Mercedes

Benz, parked diagonally to the camera lens to show off both its grill and passenger side. Cal guessed it to be of late70s or early-80s vintage. In front of the left headlight stood a beefy-looking guy — well-cut, not overweight — shaking the hand of a much slighter, balding man whom Cal soon recognized as Lucas Palmer. They were both beaming, seemingly in genuine camaraderie. The big guy was definitely a younger Chet Townsend, the owner of this cabin, whom Cal had met in a casual mailbox encounter at the end of the driveway about a year ago.

To Townsend's left, standing alone and looking away from everyone, was a delicate blonde woman in clothing that struck Cal as European in style. Across the picture, on the other side of Lucas, stood a big-boned, striking red-haired woman with a dazzling smile, lots of bracelets, and skimpy 70s-style leisure-wear. Cal examined her closely. She had the crowd-pleasing look of a celebrity, perhaps a Hollywood actress he should recognize, but he couldn't place her. She had one hand resting on the shoulder of a young dark-haired boy, perhaps ten, who was holding a Barbie doll and regarding the camera with a soulful gaze. Cal grinned and whispered, "Hey beautiful, where are you now?"

The woman's other hand was reaching out sideways for a child who had apparently slipped her grasp — a little fat girl who sat cross-legged on the ground, staring off to the side morosely, a small, shiny black purse hanging from her mouth by the strap clenched in her teeth. *Wendy*, thought Cal, and felt a twinge of pathos.

He shook off the feeling and started exploring the house.

Wendy and her father had obviously taken two adjoining rooms at the end of a long hallway. Nearly identical bags stamped with UC-DAVIS insignia lay on each bed in the rooms. It looked as if the two had just arrived when they went down to the river earlier in the day — or else they felt uncomfortable spreading out their belongings in the Townsends' tacky territory, a feeling Cal could easily understand.

In one room, the collegiate duffel bag was stuffed with a neat array of folded white Arrow shirts, a few still in their original packaging, several pairs of pants and shorts, socks — conservatively dull, carefully arranged belongings of Wendy's dad, obviously. Cal pawed through it but decided not to take anything with him. In the next room the second duffel bag was full of an insane assortment of paraphernalia: candy bars, junk food cupcakes, three crossword puzzle books, a tarot deck, a Sony Walkman and six or eight cassette tapes, all of the self-help variety. Cal recognized the smiling face of Marianne Williamson, the author of three of them. There was also another pair of the plain black cloth shoes that Wendy was wearing already, one UC-DAVIS sweatshirt, a box of instant oatmeal packages, a box of Irish Mocha Mint instant coffee mix, a package of fig bars, and still more. Cal stopped sorting through the mess when he began to feel strangely upset.

Besides, he was looking for undergarments and Wendy apparently hadn't brought any with her. That didn't make sense. He began casting his eyes about the room for another piece of luggage, spying only more items in the Townsend collection of ugly Americana. On a hunch Cal leaned over and flipped up the bedspread, revealing a rolled-up grocery bag hidden underneath the bed frame.

The bag had a mystifying weight to it. Cal unrolled the top to find what he'd been seeking: several capacious brassieres and a jumbled assortment of cheap cotton panties. Cal held up one pair with two fingers and sang in a high pitch, "Looks like she got it at Ross," grumbling afterward, "as if I don't know popular culture." He kept digging for the source of the weight and uncovered two Danielle Steele paperbacks, and finally, a plain white battery-powered vibrator.

Cal twisted the base to feel the small machine shake in his hand and commented, "Don't think she got *this* at Ross," then turned off the vibrator. He stared at it briefly, aware that everything in the bag was now unmentionable. He replaced the vibrator, books, and underwear in the same arrangement as he found them, re-rolled the top of the bag and slipped it under the bed. "Never saw it," he muttered. Barring catastrophe at the hospital, tomorrow's shopping trip was a fait accompli.

An hour later Cal was back at the Days Inn in Santa Rosa, unpacking his and Tom's clothing and toiletries. As Tom snored softly on the bed, Cal criss-crossed the room, smiling affectionately at his partner. When the necessary chores were done Cal turned a chair to face the wall and made a phone call in a muted voice, then walked to the door, opened and closed it softly behind him. He took a few steps to the next room, rapping sharply on the door.

"Wendy?" he called. "Are you in there, Wendy?"

Almost half a minute passed before Cal was prepared to knock again, but finally there was a click on the other side of the door. It opened slowly to reveal Wendy regarding him with half-closed eyes and her shoulder-length, stringy black hair in complete disarray. *Hair salon too*, Cal noted silently as Wendy mumbled, "Um, yeah?"

"Oh, I'm sorry if I woke you," Cal said softly, not meaning it. "Look, I just called the hospital and they've transferred your dad to the ICU. There's no change in his condition but that's not bad news, at this point. You can see him after seven; it's a little after six-thirty now. What say we stop by the hospital and then get some dinner? I'm starving."

Wendy's eyes were struggling to open further as she labored to process all the information given by Cal. "Um, yeah, okay," she mumbled, and then added, "I've just got to..." But when she turned to face the anonymous room she couldn't think of anything she needed to do in it.

"Brush your hair?" Cal suggested, holding up her hairbrush. "I found it in your duffel bag back at the cabin," he explained, causing Wendy to feel a twinge of embarrassment. She realized that he must have seen all the junk in her duffel bag; thank God she had hidden the other stuff!

"Oh, thanks," she said as neutrally as possible. "Yeah, I guess I really do need to brush my hair," she confessed, drawing a few strands back from her face. Stricken with the realization that she would return to this room later without her usual bedtime companionship, she turned back toward Cal just as he was about to leave. "Cal, you didn't happen to bring any of my Marianne tapes, did you?"

Cal slapped his forehead and looked genuinely crestfallen. "Oh no, I'm sorry, Wendy," he responded. "If only I'd known."

"Thass okay," she mumbled, still half-asleep, and shut the door in Cal's face. He shrugged and spoke through the door:

"Seeya in ten!"

Wendy was more awake in the car with Cal and Tom, but hardly speaking. She was struggling with an intense antipathy toward returning to the hospital. She knew this was selfish and wrong. Her dad was probably dying in there, after all, and even if he wasn't she should be keeping a perpetual vigil by his bedside, waiting for the moment when he opened his eyes. But

Wendy wanted none of it. She was perfectly content to let Cal stay in touch by phone with the proper authorities, and to be notified when it was absolutely necessary for her to do anything. Even then, she couldn't imagine what she was supposed to do if he died — or if he awakened, for that matter.

She only felt worse when they were all standing next to her father's bedside in the hospital's intensive-care unit. Perhaps because of the fluorescent lighting, Lucas looked blue and translucent to her. One side of his head was bandaged and he looked shrunken, already corpselike. She couldn't tell whether he was even breathing. The longer she looked at him the greater the anxiety she felt. She was about to go for the strap of her purse when she realized that putting it in her mouth would be a shamefully obvious thing to do in front of Tom and Cal, who were already looking at her expectantly. Was she supposed to pray out loud, or collapse in grief? Kneel and take her dad's hand, beg him to come out of it?

"Wendy, would you feel more comfortable alone with your dad?" Cal said gently, interrupting her nervous fret.

"What?" she replied, startled. "No, you can stay — I mean, oh, let's just go," she whined. "I don't like it here. They'll let us know if anything goes wrong, won't they?"

By the time they all piled back into the VW to return to downtown Santa Rosa, Wendy was weeping softly. Her anxiety about not knowing what to do had brought to mind one of the last long talks she'd had with her mother. Scarily shrunken and pale from her cancer, Flora had taken Wendy's hand and, in a wavering voice, apologized for not being the best mother in the world. Then she began instructing Wendy on social graces that she had probably forgotten to impart — when to say thank yous and you're welcomes, when to give people little gifts and when not to, when to write notes after people gave you little gifts...

Wendy had listened dutifully, wondering whether her mother's mind was going or she was deliberately repeating all this stuff she had told Wendy, who was then twenty-five, at least a hundred times before. It wasn't that Wendy was unaware of how normal people were supposed to behave; it was that she knew she wasn't normal. She was exempt by default; she was "dysfunctional," a word she had learned in therapy that seemed to summarize her whole being with scientific precision. How could she be expected to remember the social graces when she had never functioned right?

Cal and Tom had been chattering about something, maybe the great weather, but Wendy now noticed the silence pervading the car. Had they noticed she was crying? Sure enough, she felt a hand on her shoulder and Tom was speaking from the back seat, close to her ear:

"Hey Wendy, you doin' okay?"

Wendy twisted in her seat but could only get turned enough in the cramped quarters to look over at Cal, who smiled warmly at her. A new wave of tears stung her eyes as she murmured, "You guys" and trailed off, abruptly hating herself. She deliberately thunked her head against her window. "I must be, like," she sobbed, "like the worst person in the world!"

"Hey now," Cal responded sternly, "what kind of talk is that?"

"I mean it!" Wendy wailed. "I'm so awful! I didn't want to go back to the hospital and see my dad. I wouldn't have gone if you hadn't made me. He looked terrible, like he was already dead, and if he dies what am I supposed to do? My mom is already dead, you know? What am I supposed to do now? I can't do all the things that most people know how to do!"

Tom was gently squeezing her shoulder from behind as Cal tried to interrupt. "Hey Wendy, it's okay to be upset right now. You don't have to worry about what to do. We'll be right here with you all the way."

"Like that!" Wendy interrupted forcefully, "See? I haven't even thanked you guys for helping me all day long. By now I should have written you a note or something!"

Tom guffawed behind her and Cal glanced worriedly into the rearview mirror, then started to laugh as well. Surprised, Wendy abruptly stopped crying and asked "What? What's so funny?" as the men's laughter reverberated in the car.

Finally Tom reached forward to grasp her shoulder again and said, "You're absolutely right, Wendy. If I don't have a thank-you note in my hands by midnight you are really gonna be on my shit-list, girl. No Christmas party invite for you!"

Wendy looked at Cal, who was nodding and grinning along with the joke. Wendy felt a tiny smile creep onto her face. "Well, you know what I mean," she murmured. She gazed out her window with a sudden shyness, unexpectedly dazzled by the slanting rays of the setting summer sun.

Chapter 10

Lucas was flying, as much in spirit as in fact. As he drove the old, enormous anti-personnel machine — curiously equipped inside with the dashboard of his Mercedes — he had never felt so powerful, so much in control of his own destiny. After he and Patton had dropped in through the hole on top, the General had shown him there was "nothing to it" to make the tank blast away at anyone who was trouble. Firing the turret's shell cannon was simplicity itself. You just pushed in the shiny woodgrain cigarette lighter that Lucas had never used in his own car, and *kaboom*.

Lucas hadn't been able to resist a random shot even before they moved from the spot where Patton had parked to blast holes in the "real world." Standing from his seat to look out through a narrow horizontal visor situated underneath the turret, he watched eagerly as the shell he had launched blasted a ragged chunk of the horizon into deep space. "Whoa there," Patton had responded with a firm hand on his shoulder. "Let's save it for the dirty Hun. Get us out of here, soldier!"

Then Lucas had floored the accelerator and felt the mighty metal beast lurch forward on its tracks, leaping effortlessly into thin air — or was it space? — and hang there for a time-stretching moment. To Lucas the sensation of flying was delectable; Patton seemed unaffected, reaching down to pull out the trigger-lighter and use it to singe the end of a cigar he'd produced from a shirt pocket of his combat fatigues. "You like Cubans, son?" he said, clenching the fat stogie in his teeth while leaning down to peer through the slit-sight at their forward progress.

Lucas was giddily spinning the steering wheel left, then right; it seemed to make no difference in the fantastic limbo of flight. "Can't say as whether I like 'em or dislike 'em, sir," he said in the manliest tone he could muster. "We don't get a lot of 'em at Davis. Got a lot of Asians, though."

"Asians?!" Patton guffawed, pulling the cigar from his mouth and spitting rudely. "Don't believe I'd care for any damn Asian cigar."

With a flush of embarrassment Lucas realized his error; sounding manly might be trickier than he'd assumed. He stopped spinning the wheel and answered the General straight and low. "I believe you're probably right about that, sir."

Without warning there came a horrendous crash of metal against a hard surface, and Lucas was sent flying sharply upward against the hard shell of the vehicle, then crashing down to the metal-grate flooring. As the tank roughly settled itself onto a horizontal path, Lucas slowly sat up and checked himself for broken parts. Miraculously, he was unharmed. Patton was steering the tank like nothing unusual had occurred, craning his neck upward to see through the sight while still gunning the gas — a difficult stretch.

"Pop the top and see where we're headed, sonny," he barked. "I don't know this territory." Lucas clambered up half the short ladder, undid the cap latch, and shoved the heavy lid up and over. He raised himself one more step and poked his head outside the tank, only to see an unexpected yet familiar scene: Interstate 80 heading west between Sacramento and Davis, the route that Lucas had driven thousands of times in his daily commute from the house to work over the years. The tank was bombing along at a surprising clip, keeping up with most of the automobiles. Lucas had never known these awkward beasts could do 60-plus.

Patton's driving was aggressive, to say the least. If a slowpoke car in front of them didn't get out of their way, he simply rammed it off the road. Lucas winced and held on for dear life when the tank came up rapidly behind an ancient, ailing pickup truck and simply rolled over it, crushing the vehicle and whomever was inside it. Lucas thought about suggesting to the General that he could take it easy. But then he remembered that they were on a warpath he had chosen himself, and there were always some peripheral casualties in war.

With the warm California wind whipping his face, Lucas smiled and felt proud of himself for remembering to hang tough. While he and Patton were on much better terms than when they first met, he still wouldn't want to cross the old man as long as he had a lot of firepower at his disposal.

Soon Lucas saw his familiar exit to the university ahead, and shouted down to Patton to veer right. As the General took them off the main highway, Lucas slipped back down into the tank's musty inner chamber, pulling the tank lid after him and relatching it.

"We're getting close, sir," he announced excitedly.

Patton gave him a cigar-clenching grin and stepped away from the primitive steel seat behind the swanky dashboard.

"All right sonny, take her in. It's showtime!"

Lucas resumed his control of the steering wheel and tried to drive more carefully than Patton, although it required standing to look through the slit-sight while steering. Like Patton, he couldn't reach the gas pedal at the same time. Patton finally said, "Here we go, son," and mashed down the accelerator himself, freeing Lucas to navigate, albeit at top speed. "Goddamn engineers," Patton fumed, "couldn't design a shithouse if their lives depended on it."

"Stop, sir!" Lucas cried, as the tank splashed violently through a bucolic creek on the campus at Davis, scattering lunchtime picnickers, sunbathers, and studious readers alike. The tank lurched to a resting position with the gun turret pointed squarely at the faculty lounge. Lucas considered taking out the whole building, then thought better of it. He felt certain that Royal Martin would exit the courtyard door of the lounge at any moment. When the bastard was clear of innocent bystanders and taxpayer-funded facilities, Lucas would nail him with surgical precision. Clasping the handgrips of the gun periscope with clammy hands, Lucas peered intently through the telescopic lens and waited with bated breath.

Sure enough, momentarily the old teacher stepped through the courtyard door, pausing to shade his eyes against the punishing Davis sun and rake a few strands of hair over his glistening scalp. To Lucas' glee, the absent-minded professor then began walking away from the building onto the grassy hillside, straight down the slope toward the tank as if he couldn't see a deadly bull elephant in his path. Lucas reached down to finger the lighter, counting under his breath *one, two, three*. When Martin was so large in the periscope's crosshairs that Lucas could count his liver spots, Lucas shoved in the lighter. The tank rocked backwards, the charge exploding so loudly that it seemed to have gone off right inside the tank's cramped quarters. A shell screamed toward Dr. Martin's heart; in a second, he was blown to bits.

"Bingo!" shouted Patton. Lucas slumped from the periscope with his ears ringing, feeling nauseated. Patton grabbed him roughly by the shoulder and shouted, "Get off your duff, sonny, and let's get out there to confirm the kill! This will be the first one on your jacket. By God it looked dead to rights to me!"

After clambering out the top and jumping off the side of the tank, Lucas' every step toward his shattered victim felt increasingly heavy and slow. The panicky excitement of running down and targeting his prey had rapidly evolved into a guilty dread, and Lucas lagged behind the hustling General. When he caught up with him, Patton was standing in a rough circle of scattered straw and blasted earth. Falling from his hands were ragged fragments of Royal Martin's clothing, but Lucas couldn't see the blood or bone fragments he had feared — just loose filaments of straw and an ochre dust in the air. Patton looked crestfallen.

Lucas came abreast of the General and picked up some blasted yellow grass himself. "What the devil?" he murmured.

"It's that damn Rommel," Patton replied grimly.

"What?" Lucas said, bewildered.

"His old Straw Man Gambit," Patton explained unhelpfully. "Dammit, I read his book — I should have seen it coming. Tricky Hun bastard."

Lucas let the last bits of straw tumble from his fingers, trying not to let the General see that he felt relieved. He turned about to conceal his face and saw Flora sitting on the ground six feet away, the picnic basket full of diamonds by her side.

"Well dear," she said sardonically, "are you happy now?"

Lucas dropped to the ground beside Flora in a cross-legged squat and sighed heavily; he felt utterly exhausted. Patton was shaking his fist at the sky and kicking up tufts of grass as he stalked back to the tank. He clambered inside, shut the top and began backing the machine away from the married couple on the grass. Lucas turned to Flora and said, "I don't know what to feel, Flora. What's really going on here? I think I'm just not getting it."

Flora smiled tensely, revealing the same tentative vulnerability she used to show when she had to ask Lucas for money to stage her New Age scripts. "Well, honey," she said in her most reasonable tone, "I told you when you arrived that this is your show. You're the writer, director, and producer. I'm not the type to tell you how to run your own production, of course, but really — *that man*," she hissed, tilting her head toward the receding tank. "Must we keep running into him when we have so much work to do?"

Lucas was about to protest that he had no control over Patton's appearances when Flora spoke again, staring at the ground and nervously picking at blades of grass. "But I guess you have your reasons to be angry, considering everything." She raised her head to look straight-on at Lucas, her lovely hazel eyes full of shame, and added, "After all, I suppose I should be grateful that you haven't come gunning for *me*."

The pained expression on Flora's face brought to Lucas' mind a sequence of events that he would just as soon have forgotten. He felt the nearness of an ancient, almost overpowering bitterness, and an equally powerful reluctance to revisit it. Without rancor, he gazed helplessly at Flora and asked, "We don't have to go there, do we?"

"Absolutely," she replied soberly. "Believe me, I'd rather not.

But for Wendy..." she trailed off. She pronounced their daughter's name in the same tone they'd always used between them, as a shorthand signal of all the pathos and exasperation they had felt as failing parents.

CHAPTER 11

BY THE time the trio in the classic VW had returned to downtown Santa Rosa, everyone was in high spirits. The uncomfortable scene at the hospital was seemingly forgotten. After parking the car, Cal, Tom, and Wendy ambled around town as if they were the oldest of friends, Tom keeping a friendly arm around Wendy's shoulders as they walked.

Behind the casual conversation Wendy was marveling at two things about Tom: the matter-of-fact way he touched everyone, even her, almost constantly; and his extraordinary capacity to be more than one person in the course of a day. It wasn't just the way he spoke in other voices. Wendy was more impressed with how he had changed from being hostile and petulant when they first met, only hours ago, to being warm and gracious now. Perhaps some would call it instability, but to Wendy this kind of flexibility in one's character was incomprehensible. While she often felt like she was riding a rickety roller-coaster of emotions (especially today), she was the same old Wendy whenever the ride came to a stop. And that Wendy was static, unchanging, veritably mountainous in her sense of self. Over the years she had tried every self-help technique in the books because she suspected that she, Wendy Palmer, would always be fat, anxious, and unhappy.

But for the moment these deep concerns were in the background. She was enjoying the rare company of men who treated her like an equal, a pal. Although they had some difficulty settling on a restaurant for dinner because Cal sniffed disdainfully at every place they investigated, they finally settled on a boisterous Mexican eatery called the Cantina in the center Of town, just under the golden cupola of the Empire Building. Tom said he thought the joint looked "happy" and Cal said he supposed he could survive it.

Wendy usually regarded Mexican restaurants as caloric minefields that she must gingerly step around. But she'd eaten almost nothing so far that day, so she could afford an indulgence. Tom was right: the place was buzzing with young professionals drinking in the bar, noisy families laughing at big tables, well-mannered staff running in every direction. Wendy always liked this kind of place; it made her feel unnoticeable.

As soon as they were seated Cal ordered a big pitcher of sangria and asked for lots of chips. Wendy began to feel giddy, as if she'd been invited to a party. Chips and guacamole arrived almost immediately, but the men seemed far more interested in food than Wendy was. By now she was so curious about Tom that she asked, just like a normal person would, "So, Tom, what kind of work do you do?"

The question caught Tom unprepared; he had been busy constructing a guacamole sandwich between two of the largest tortilla chips he could fish from the basket. His mouth was stuffed and crackling as Cal filled in, "Tom here is the moneybags of the family. Mr. Whizkid, the Stockbroker Phenom."

Wendy's eyes widened. "Really?" she exclaimed. The job

sounded so grown-up that she had a hard time seeing the energetic, childlike Tom fitting in to that world. "So you're like, a big success?"

Tom, trying to swallow, waved dismissively but Cal pressed on. "You bet. Everyone wonders how Tom anticipates the market so well. If he keeps it up the SEC is going to investigate him to find out where he gets his inside tips." Cal snapped a chip in half and swallowed it seemingly without bothering to chew. "The thing is, they probably wouldn't want to know how he does it. I'm sure I don't."

"Whereas Cal," Tom intervened, finally getting his mouth free, "keeps our karmic accounts balanced. He runs the AIDS Task Force in Oakland by day and harangues the city's agencies about their environmental sins by night. If you want your politics corrected, Cal's your man." Tom finished his description with a slap on the table, as if he'd scored a decisive point, then added, "So what do you do, Wendy?"

Cringing, Wendy remembered why she usually didn't start this kind of conversation; it always led back to her. "Oh, just dumb stuff. Temp secretary jobs, things like that. I don't work right now 'cuz . . ." she paused to devise an excuse and abruptly decided it was too much effort. "I'm virtually unemployable," she declared with a hint of pride. "I get too upset to work for very long."

Cal curled his lower lip under his top teeth and looked uncomfortable while Tom posed a direct, almost cutting inquiry. "So how do you get by? You live with your dad?"

"Why, yes," Wendy answered, surprised by Tom's deduction. "We have this really big house in Sacramento that belongs to my grandmother Agnes. Since my mother died, it's half-empty even with me there... Dad has tenure at Davis," she concluded, hoping that explained everything somehow.

Their perky young waitress arrived and took orders; thereafter Tom excused himself to the restroom. Cal launched into a critical review of the restaurant decor until Wendy, aware of the sparks flying between her companions, interjected sorrowfully, "I hope I'm not screwing up your weekend."

"Nah," Cal replied, "we were just taking a little breather from work. We're glad to help out until — until your dad is okay. No biggie."

Wendy leaned closer and spoke in a stage whisper, keeping an eye on the path that Tom had taken to the restroom. "But Tom told me earlier that you had a lot to talk about. He said it was a 'make-it-or-break-it' weekend."

Cal snorted and transferred a whole handful of chips to a small plate in front of him. "Oh, that's just Tom," he replied dismissively. "Every weekend is make-it-or-break-it for him. We're fine."

Wendy regarded Cal doubtfully as Tom bounded up behind him, clapped him on the shoulders as if they were indeed the happiest couple in the world, and returned to his seat with a big smile. "So, Wendy," he inquired, "who's the light of your life?"

"Tom!" Cal barked.

"What?"

"Maybe Wendy doesn't want to share every detail of her private life with us just yet." Cal's tone was firm, fatherly.

"Oh," Tom replied in a small voice, looking genuinely contrite before winking at Wendy and murmuring, "Never mind."

But Wendy felt eager to talk. She had discussed the problem of Wayne with two therapists, her father, the weekly housecleaner, and her favorite coffee-shop waitress for months without being able to decide what to do about him. Without knowing why, she felt that Cal and Tom might be able to offer stunning new insights, even a final solution to the number three or four problem in her life — after her weight, her having nothing to do most of the time, and her emotions, depending on which way she ordered them all on any particular day.

"I sort of have a boyfriend," she began uncertainly.

"Sort of?" Cal replied, glancing sternly at Tom.

"His name is Wayne Stoughton," she said, and then launched into her standard twenty-minute love-problem litany that she had delivered so many times in the last two years. Even though the recitation invariably wearied her, she always felt compelled to get all the way through it without interruption. When the food arrived about five minutes in, she hardly paused to look at it, even as Cal and Tom dug in. She told them how she had met Wayne, a divorced car salesman, when she and her dad took his old Mercedes in to look at trade-ins, and how he had called her for two weeks before she consented to go out, and how he had taken her to the fanciest places and treated her like a queen, except for practically forcing sex on the second date. How he always talked about his wife and whether they should get back together, how he talked about attractive women all the time, how he made fun of her sometimes but sometimes took her camping, which no one else, not even her parents, had ever done — unless you counted all those fat camps she'd been sent to as a teenager. How Wayne had been more remote the past few months, snapping at her and slapping her and then apologizing profusely, practically begging for sex. How she suspected that he had several other women most of the time, including his ex-wife. How she didn't know what she felt and couldn't decide what to do...

"I can tell you what to do," Tom broke in just before Wendy's litany was complete.

"To-om," Cal said in a warning tone.

"What?" Wendy asked softly.

Tom picked up Wendy's fork and handed it to her. "First, eat your enchilada. It's getting cold. Then — *run*, girl! Put some permanent distance between you and this loser."

"Dammit, Tom!" Cal exploded. "This is none of your..."

"No, wait!" Wendy interjected, surprising herself with her willingness to confront Cal. "How do you know, Tom? Do you hear something?"

Tom shook his head and grimaced. "Yeah, what I hear is that you're miserable hanging around this guy. He's cheating on you, he hits you, he insults you! I mean, what's the point, Wendy? Why put up with all this?"

Wendy felt tears sting her eyes, feeling exposed and foolish — but then she remembered the singular virtue of Wayne that she had told no one before. She didn't know why, but the day had made her feel that the big container of long-held secrets within her was beginning to tip over. Things were going to start spilling out whether she liked it or not.

"He makes me come," she stated plainly. "Nothing else does."

Cal hacked violently, choking on some food he'd just swallowed, and turned aside in his chair to spit into his napkin. Tom laughed gaily and pounded his boyfriend's back a couple times until Cal resumed his normal posture and smiled weakly at Wendy, his eyes watering.

Tom asked Wendy, "How often?"

"Oh Jesus," Cal whimpered, closing his eyes as if he were praying over his plate.

Wendy gazed at the corner of the restaurant ceiling and seemed to be calculating. "Well, we haven't been having sex very often. So, maybe once a month."

Tom shook his head matter-of-factly. "Forget it. Lose him. You can find somebody with a better average than that." He winked and nudged Cal with an elbow, smiling wickedly. Cal opened his eyes, blushed, and busied himself with his food.

Wendy sat back in her chair and felt something shift deep within her, like tectonic plates whose unseen movements beneath the earth can change whole landscapes on the surface. She suddenly knew it was settled; she would leave Wayne for good. She didn't know how it had come about, but there was a rare certainty in front of her: *You can find somebody better.* Despite all the advice she had solicited and received for several years, this radical thought had never occurred to her before.

"Thank you, Tom. That's really helpful. No one else has ever given me such clear advice."

"Really?" he replied incredulously.

"My therapist always tells me to stay in touch with my feelings and then I'll know what to do. That *never* works. And my dad..."

"What does he say?" Cal asked, having recollected himself enough to be curious.

Wendy smiled sadly. "Well, I think my dad brought me to Guerneville so I could meet a nice gay woman. That's because the last time we talked about Wayne, I got mad and said I might as well become a lesbian. My dad tends to take things literally," she sighed, and finally took a bite of her cooled dinner.

"Well, the important thing is that he cares," Cal said diplomatically, repressing a smile. "Which reminds me," he added, anxious to steer the conversation into new territory, "is there anyone else we should notify about your dad's accident? Like your brother?"

"My brother?" Wendy asked in surprise. "What brother?"

"Oh," Cal said, looking embarrassed as Tom squinted at him curiously. "I thought — well, I saw this picture in the Townsends' house, of them and your family. You looked about ten years old? This woman who I assumed was your mom was standing behind a boy about your age."

Wendy gasped and covered her mouth, swallowing hard. "Oh my God, that picture! I made my parents get rid of our copy. I was freaking out because of that car. I thought Dad would kill us all driving too fast!"

"But the little boy is...?" Cal asked quizzically.

"Oh, that's Pierre, the Townsends' son. We had just met them a few weeks before, although Dad knew Mr. Townsend from college. From the moment we met them, Pierre seemed to like my mom better than his own. He's a dancer and my mom was in the theatre, you know, so they kind of gravitated toward each other. His mother is French, and sort of cold." Wendy's voice trailed off as she seemed to become lost in memory.

Cal was still intent. "Is there no one else we should notify?"

Wendy blinked. "Well, there's my Gramma Aggie —" she paused to give a nod to Tom, who looked at her uncomprehending — "but she's in Munich or someplace like that. I don't know how to find her, at least not until I get back home. So I can't think of anybody except... Mr. Townsend!"

"Yes?" Cal asked.

"Mr. Townsend is my dad's best friend, I guess," Wendy said thoughtfully, as if she'd never recognized the relationship before.

Chapter 12

"ALL RIGHT," Lucas said decisively, taking Flora's hands in his own. "For Wendy, then." He looked deeply into his wife's eyes and let his consciousness begin drifting into the past, using Flora's face as a guidepost in time. Like an old elevator, his awareness jarred to a stop on a Sunday afternoon in 1978, when he was driving his wife and daughter around Sacramento in the ancient Chevy Nova his mother had given him in college more than a decade before.

Ostensibly the family was out shopping for a new car. In fact Lucas was driving aimlessly, wandering over the landscape in the same way he would lead his students on survey trips. Travelling the earth's surface, even in a small circuit, always calmed his nerves, and they needed calming after a full morning of arguing with Flora. She had recently begun a campaign to convince Lucas that they should tell Wendy "the whole truth": how she had been an accident and her birth date had been falsified at Agnes' command. Flora was convinced that the lie had something to do with Wendy's adjustment problems in school. One teacher had proclaimed Wendy "naturally bright, but so emotionally unbalanced as to be virtually uneducable."

But Lucas was unconvinced, and resolutely so. "She doesn't know a thing about it," he had kept saying to Flora, "and she's better off that way." He felt that telling a nine (ten)-year-old girl — who was already in a teary panic half the time — that she was an accident would be a recipe for complete disaster. Not to mention that he had sworn a pledge to his mother to uphold the secret forever, in exchange for the financial rescue she had executed when he and Flora got into trouble.

But after a morning of battling head-on with his fiery wife, Lucas wondered morosely if he'd really been rescued after all. It felt cruelly unfair to find himself in a power struggle between his mother and his wife, and he wondered ruefully how his life had been reduced to such a banal circumstance. At least he had weaned himself financially from Agnes after taking the position at Davis — except for the house they were living in, of course.

After Wendy had come home from a perfunctory Sunday school class and they had all shared a stone-silent lunch at the kitchen nook table, Lucas leaned over to Wendy and said with false enthusiasm, "Let's go get a new car!"

Wendy opened a mouth half-full of peanut butter and mushily replied, "I like our old car. It goes nice and slow."

"Wendy, don't talk with your mouth full," Flora commanded coldly. "Get your purse and let's go. I've certainly had enough of our old car."

But as soon as they had all piled into the rusting vehicle and Flora had noisily slammed her passenger door the three times required for it to latch, Lucas had frozen in his seat. He had no idea of how to buy a car. This was one of the manly tasks for which he had somehow received no cultural training.

As he sat with his hands in his lap — Flora peering at him with curiosity and impatience — Lucas realized that this gap in his masculine education had to do with his father.

Jack Palmer died when Lucas was twelve, and the boy had seen precious little of him before then. A roving engineer for Standard Oil, the senior Palmer had criss-crossed the world multiple times at his superiors' every whim, always promising his wife and son that he would retire early with quite a little nest egg to share with them. Lucas supposed that his father's travels had a lot to do with his career choice, for when he was little he spent hours after dinners with his mom poring over world maps and National Geographics, trying to visualize his dad's peregrinations. Lucas would often fall asleep afterward to dream that he was flying with his dad all around the globe. In his dreams the little boy could somehow see all the way around the earth at once; it was whole, complete, and translucent, like a bright jewel suspended in space.

When Lucas was twelve, his father did come home for an extended hiatus from work, looking pale and overweight. He keeled over dead from a massive coronary within the week.

Lucas sighed and clapped the steering wheel with both hands, smiling gamely at Flora and murmuring, "Well, let's go then." Flora was shaking her head at yet another of her husband's unexplained silences. While he could stand up to his wife sometimes, Lucas felt certain that he would be so much chum for the brightly-clad sharks that circled on Sacramento's auto row. He would probably get ripped off, and Flora would watch it happen with smug satisfaction — unless she stepped in to use her not-inconsiderable feminine wiles to throw off the salesmen. She still had a way with men, that was for sure.

Thus, as usual, hesitation and ambivalence were behind the wheel as Lucas drove around the outskirts of California's capital city. When Flora started giving him her let's-get-on-with-it look — she had found herself an involuntary wanderer more than once in her husband's company — he announced cheerily, "I think we're getting close now!" Then he heard a faint ripping noise, the sound of something falling like raindrops on the back seat, and an ear-splitting wail from Wendy.

"Waa-aanh!" she screeched. "Mommy, it broke again!"

Flora twisted in her seat and regarded her daughter with restrained hostility. "For God's sake, Wendy, I must have told you a hundred times to stop yanking on that necklace!" Lucas felt a bump against the back of his seat, and knew without looking that Wendy was reaching down to the floorboard, looking for her diamonds. On Wendy's last birthday, Agnes had given her a necklace of huge, fake plastic diamonds with a card saying, "For an elegant young lady, from Grandmother Agnes." Wendy had refused to go out of the house without the necklace ever since. But once it was around her neck she pulled at it compulsively, and the original flimsy chain that linked the diamonds had broken in no time. Flora kept re-stringing the necklace with strong thread, but Wendy was wearing that out every couple weeks as well.

As Wendy rustled about gathering all the plastic beads, Flora reaching awkwardly between the seats to help, Lucas finally pulled the car onto the main drag where all the major auto dealers hawked their wares. Halfway down the first block, a huge Macy's-parade-style balloon of a striped tiger bobbed in the light spring breeze over a crowded parking lot festooned with multi-colored flags and a huge banner that read GRAND OPENING. As the car came abreast of the entrance the sounds of a Dixieland band could be heard. Lucas rolled down his window as the car rolled to a stop by the sidewalk.

"Look Wendy," he cried, hoping to distract his daughter

from her latest upset, "a big party!"

"Hunh?" Wendy replied from somewhere behind and beneath Lucas; then he felt a violent push against his seat back. "Oww!" Wendy yelped, and began crying. "I hit my head!"

"Oh, hush dear," Flora sighed. Lucas shook his head and returned his attention to the festivities in the car lot. The band had stopped playing abruptly, and the crowd was being led in a countdown by a clownish figure in a red-white-and-blue Uncle Sam suit. Fifteen feet to either side of the clown were two bikini-clad young women cocking their hips suggestively and pointing up toward a long rectangular sign, covered with a white cloth, that topped the width of the plate-glass windows fronting the auto dealer's building.

"Four — three — two — one — *bingo*!" Uncle Sam bellowed nonsensically, and the bikini girls stepped over to pull on gold ceremonial ropes that brought down the cloth covering the signs, revealing large block neon letters flashing the legend TOWNSEND MERCEDES-BENZ. As a big man in a silvery suit stepped over to accept a cigar handed to him with a flourish by Uncle Sam, Lucas craned his neck out the window of his dingy Nova and murmured, "No, couldn't be..."

In a flash he was out of the car and striding into the crowd of onlookers, leaving Flora to yell uselessly after him, "Lu-uke! I don't think we can afford a Mercedes, dear!"

A few minutes had passed by the time Flora and Wendy got all the plastic diamonds collected and stowed safely in Wendy's purse, then got out of the car and threaded their way through the crowd to find Lucas. He was standing just to the rear of a man in a silvery suit, whose square back and shock of dark hair looked faintly familiar to Flora. When he turned to face them she gasped. Lucas was extending his hand, saying, "Chet?

Do you remember me?"

The big man with bright eyes leaned over toward Lucas with a dazzling salesman's smile and said "Why, sure, Mister..." and then his smile collapsed. He narrowed his eyes and said in a near-whisper, "Palmer? Filth — Luke? Luke Palmer?"

"Yes, that's right," Lucas replied, a crafty grin spreading across his face.

"Lucas Palmer!" Chet Townsend suddenly boomed, rapidly regaining his com-posure and reaching out to embrace Lucas with one arm around his shoulders. "Why, you old son of a gun!" In turning to embrace Lucas, Chet came face to face with Flora, who seemed to be blanching, her eyes darting left and right as if seeking an escape route. "Flora," Chet said neutrally, adding as he nodded toward Lucas, "Or, Mrs. Palmer, of course."

Flora decorously extended a hand and said stiffly, "Why hello, Chet. It's been a long time."

"Long time is hardly the word for it!" Chet laughed raucously, as if he had said something humorous. "Luke, you old son of a gun. Are you living in Sacramento these days?"

"Yessir," Lucas replied in an unusually boisterous tone, the crafty grin not quite removed from his visage. "I'm in the Geography department at Davis. I didn't know you were here too."

"Just blew into town, Luke. Been working in my dad's business up in Eureka ever since college, but I finally got up the gumption to do my own thing. Can you imagine living your whole life in Eureka? I promised the wife we'd get out of the sticks someday, and here we are!" Chet gestured grandly toward the newly revealed sign proclaiming his dealership, and asked, "So what do you think, Luke?"

"Pretty impressive," Lucas replied, jutting his chin manfully. "What business is your dad in, Chet?"

"Chevy dealer," he sneered. "Didn't want to live my life that way, Luke. I'm sure you understand. Say, it sounds like that education did you some good, hunh? A professor! Damn, maybe I shoulda cracked a book or two back in Chico."

Lucas shrugged his shoulders and said, "Well, you'll probably make a bundle here, what with all the politicos in town. I'm afraid I'm just in the market for a Chevy myself."

Chet shot a glance at Flora, who was bending over to point Wendy's attention at the tiger balloon floating above them. He returned his gaze to Lucas with his eyes brightening, his chest rapidly swelling out like a rooster's. "Nonsense, Professor Palmer," he boomed, "a man in your position deserves a vehicle that reflects your status in life. There's too much hullabaloo going on here today, but why don't you drop by next week and I'll show you the latest models myself. I'm the boss, you know — I'll cut you a good deal for old times' sake." Chet was looking at Flora again, who gave him a perfunctory smile.

"Aw, Chet," Lucas protested with an envious look over the field of shiny luxury automobiles before them, "I could afford about half of one of these."

"Lu-uke," Chet intoned, pulling the smaller man closer to him with the arm that had yet to leave his shoulders, "I said I would cut you a deal, okay? Just give me a call tomorrow and we'll set something up. Don't waste any more of this beautiful day wandering around looking at damn Chevys." Chet finally released Lucas and bent down with his hands on his knees to grin at Wendy. "So, is this little beauty yours, Luke?"

Wendy squinted up at Chet and whined, "I like our old car."

"Ha, ha, ha!" Chet barked, straightening up and speaking with a look directly into Flora's eyes. "She's a sassy little one, isn't she?"

"Is your family here, Chet?" Flora asked quietly.

"Why, sure," he replied. "Monique is around here somewhere, and my son Pierre..." he raised a hand to his eyes to survey the crowded lot, then waved and yelled "Hey there, bub!" to someone he recognized.

"Monique?" Lucas said quizzically. "You mean Monique from France?"

"Hey, you old son of a gun, you remember, don't you? Yeah, I married an import myself!" Chet laughed. Lucas cast his eyes to the ground, recalling the attractive but chilly French exchange student whom Chet had begun squiring around the Chico campus just when Lucas was being given the boot from the frat house. He was about to ask Chet something when a slender young boy carrying a Barbie doll slipped through the crowd and grabbed one of Chet's stocky legs, crying, "Dad-dee! Dad-dee!"

"Hey, kiddo!" Chet said jovially before bending over and grabbing the doll from his son's hands to hide it behind his back. In a low tone that Lucas could barely pick up, Chet admonished the boy: "Pierre, I told you to leave your damn doll in my desk until we get back home." Then he straightened up, his face slightly reddened, and announced to Lucas and Flora, "Yeah, this is my boy Pierre. He's almost ten."

A pale, slight blonde in a floral dress and a sunhat appeared beside Chet and said, "Cherie?"

"Oh, and here's the wife!" Chet added, looking more uncomfortable by the moment. "Monique, meet my old buddy from college, Luke Palmer. This is his wife Flora, and their little girl...?"

"Wendy," Flora said.

"Wendy," Chet responded, nodding. "Looks like we could

have a couple playmates here, eh Luke?"

"He's ten?" Lucas asked curiously, squinting at Chet, whose eyes briefly flickered in response. At that moment Lucas knew for sure that he and Chet Townsend had more in common than they would speak of that day. He decided on the spot that he would indeed give Chet a call the next day. Then he cast a look at Monique, who was smiling painfully and extending a tiny hand toward Flora.

"Enchanté," she mewed. "Eet's always nice to meet ze old friends of my husband."

ONE week later, the Palmer family had returned to Townsend Mercedes-Benz to pick up Lucas' brand-new silver sedan. For Lucas it was a miraculous acquisition in several respects. First, it was a miracle that Lucas ever saw Chet Townsend again, given Flora's fierce resistance to the idea. The evening following the unexpected reunion, Flora had shut the door on Wendy in the TV room and gone to work on Lucas in the kitchen.

"He's a creep, always was a creep, and I know he'll rip you off!" she'd angrily proclaimed.

"Oh, I'm in this just for fun," Lucas replied mildly. "I want to see if I can give him a hard time in exchange for all those hard times he gave me back in school. 'Old college buddies,' he said. Did you hear that, honey?"

"And exactly how are you going to give Chet Townsend a hard time?" Flora challenged.

"Not sure yet. I'm thinking on it."

"He's a creep. I wish you'd just forget about it, Luke. If you don't call back, he'll certainly forget about you."

The second miracle was that when Lucas did meet Chet the following Wednesday, the car salesman seemed intent on humiliating himself without the professor's instigation. Chet was unexpectedly downcast as they sat in his half-furnished office, his numerous athletic award plaques from high school and college scattered on the floor, leaning against the walls. After short pleasantries Chet motioned toward the plaques and said, "There it is, Luke. All I have to show for my academic career, besides a lousy biz-ad degree. All I did at Chico was drink and party — well, hell, it's not like you don't know about it. You had the good sense to stick to your studies, and look where you are now."

Lucas' vague scheme to needle Chet was rapidly dissolving, and he didn't quite know how to respond. "Well, Chet, I — it looks like you've got some blessings to count. Look at this big place you've got!"

"Yeah, right," Chet replied bitterly. "You mean, look at the big place that belongs to my daddy and the bank. I'm just a caretaker, and if I don't move some of these crates fast, I won't even be that for long."

Now Lucas felt guilty. "Well look, Chet, it was very nice of you to invite me back here, but I'm probably just wasting your time. Like I said, I can't afford..."

Chet waved him off and leaned forward in his high-backed leather chair, the springs squeaking with his movement. "So how is Flora doing, Luke?"

"Uh, Flora? She's all right, I guess. You know she didn't finish at Chico because we, uh, decided to get married, and then we had Wendy, you know — one year after that, I mean. Anyway, she put herself into night classes and got her drama degree and a teaching certificate. She teaches drama and English at a high school now."

"Well, that's just great, Luke," Chet replied with a sigh.

"Boy, you're a winner in the marriage department too. Flora's still a knockout, just like she always was."

"Yes," Lucas said hesitantly, unused to guy-talk about his own wife. "So you married Monique, hey?"

"Yeah, yeah," Chet said softly, and then lowered his voice to a confidential murmur. "Look, I think I can be square with an old college pal, can't I? Fact is that Pierre was a little bit of a surprise, if you know what I mean. Of course I love the both of them just like the devil, you know, but what the hell? Nothing like French fries every night of the week, eh? Ha, ha, HA!" By now Chet was barking harshly just like he had done at Wendy on Sunday, and Lucas felt ill at ease. Fortunately Chet stood, literally shaking with his weird hilarity, and motioned Lucas toward the show floor outside his office.

The final miracle had occurred less than half an hour later, after Chet had repeatedly urged Lucas to "pick the car of your dreams." Lucas had kept deferring, thinking that Chet was setting him up for humiliation after all. But the professor finally took a seat in the silver sedan he'd spotted when he first walked in the door, and settling into the plush driver's seat, said, "Ah yes, if I was going to live out my fantasies, Chet — this would be the one."

Chet had confidently motioned Lucas back into his office, rustled through some papers in his desk drawer, then took a fancy fountain pen and wrote something on a TOWNSEND MERCEDES-BENZ letterhead with a flourish. He folded it in half and pushed it across the desk to Lucas. "Let's see if this starts a conversation," he said conspiratorially. "And remember — I don't have to take this to the guy in the front office, because I'm the guy."

Lucas reached tentatively for the paper and unfolded it

partway, peeking at the inscribed figure. It was exactly half the list price Lucas had seen in the car's window. "You can't mean this, Chet!" he exclaimed.

"You old son of a gun," Chet responded heartily. "All right, I'll take off another thousand for that piece of Chevy crap you're driving now. No offense intended, of course."

"What?!" Lucas sputtered. "No, Chet, you're kidding around with me, aren't you?" He felt a flush of anger rise on the back of his neck.

"Never," Chet forcefully declaimed. "I never kid around with an offer. That's as solid as my brick fireplace, old buddy."

"But how?" Lucas protested.

"Hey, don't worry about the how. That's my department. You just worry about where you're gonna park this beauty. I hope you've got a garage, Luke, cause she don't deserve to be out in the sun and the rain like mere mortal automobiles." Chet smiled broadly and got out of his chair, walking around his desk to sit on one corner, closer to Lucas. "Look, old buddy," he continued in an almost soulful tone, "I know there must be some scores you'd like to settle with me from those days in Chico. There were times I was a perfect horse's ass, I know that — especially all that business with Flora?"

"Yeah?" Lucas replied helplessly, speechless, his eyes still riveted on the piece of paper in his shaking hand. "Yeah, well, all that stuff. Luke, you know I'm not a smart man. There are times I could use a smart man to talk to, and you were always the smartest I knew. I gave you such a hard time back then because I envied you, buddy — you kept your eyes on the prize and you got the beautiful girl, you know? Anyway..." Chet paused to take a deep breath, as if he might be near tears, then continued.

"Well, what I'm trying to say is, there's some things I did in college that really fucked up my life and I can't change them all now. But maybe there's a few things I can fix. If you really like this car, you know, and it helps you feel a little better about that shit I did — well, Luke, I'd just be proud to call you my friend." Chet abruptly rose from his seat on the corner of the desk, and went over to the wall to pick up one of his plaques, keeping his back to Lucas.

"Well, sure, Chet," Lucas mumbled, "I was never a guy to hold grudges." He glanced at the figure on paper again, turned in his chair to peer at the Mercedes on the show floor, and exclaimed, "Jesus, this is great!"

And thus, on the next Sunday Lucas had dragged an unwilling Flora and an even more stubborn Wendy back to the Townsend dealership for a family portrait in front of their new car. Monique and the Townsends' son were back again as well. The parents' attempts to corral the two kids into friendship resulted in Wendy morosely watching Flora and Pierre create an improvisational play about the fantastic life of the boy's Barbie doll. When Chet and Lucas were through positioning the automobile in just the right spot for a photograph, they gathered everyone in front of one gleaming fender while a Townsend salesman readied his camera.

Instead of going to his own mother, Pierre backed himself up against Flora, who smiled and placed a hand on his left shoulder. Standing under her mom's other hand, Wendy glared sidewise at the Mercedes as if it were a deadly serpent and wailed, "Is this a fast car, Daddy?"

It was Chet who answered, "You better believe it, doll!" and Wendy shrieked, dropping to a squat on the ground and clenching her purse strap in her teeth just as the shutter clicked.

Monique — standing off to the side of her beaming husband who clasped the hand of an equally beaming Lucas — had just turned her eyes eastward, toward Europe.

That evening, Flora seemed unusually quiet as Lucas found a series of excuses to go outside and check the car under the vinyl cover Chet had lent him in lieu of a garage. Finally, in bed under the half-light of a reading lamp, Lucas noticed Flora's demeanor and asked her if she was okay.

"Yes, sweetie," she said balefully, "I guess so. That Pierre is such a nice boy, isn't he?"

"Yeah," Lucas laughed, "a little too nice for Chet's taste, I think. He's really worried about that doll."

"Oh, Chet," Flora replied, as if the salesman were in the room with them. "Luke... are you going to be big friends with him now?"

"Well, I don't know, honey. He's going a long way to even things up between us. I was surprised by that, I really was. He even apologized for 'that business with Flora,' believe it or not?"

"He what?" Flora blurted, obviously alarmed.

"You know, all that grief he gave me when we met, about how I stole you from him and everything."

"And that's it?"

Lucas felt a sudden disturbance in his gut. "Well, yes, I suppose so. What do you mean, honey?"

"Oh my God," Flora whispered, and sat up in bed to look Lucas straight in the eyes. "Look, honey, I know I've been needling you about our telling Wendy the whole truth, and it's probably because..."

"Because?"

Flora swallowed hard. "Because I haven't told you the whole truth about me. I thought I'd never have to, but now that Chet has shown up, I might as well tell you before it slips out in some worse way. You see, honey, Chet and I once — well, there was a weekend when you were away on one of those field trips, and I ran into Chet and he got me drinking and — I mean, he didn't make me drink, I'm not saying he forced me into anything, I was just lonely and we were having a good time.... oh shit," she finished mournfully, burying her face in the pillow.

Lucas felt his breath go shallow, but he remembered that he was a reasonable man and there was a brand-new Mercedes sitting in the driveway. He forced a couple deep breaths and composed himself, searching carefully for just the right tone to conceal his inner turmoil.

"Well, honey, this is certainly a shock. But whatever happened was a long time ago and we were kids then. I mean, we weren't engaged or anything. So you had a date, and things just got out of control, right? Is that what you're saying?"

"Yes!" Flora quickly responded, rising up from her pillow, wiping away a tear. "Yes, that's exactly it. We were all pretty crazy back then, huh?"

"Yeah, sure," Lucas replied, still managing to keep his voice even. "Everybody was a little wild. I suppose I can't blame you for that kind of thing, can I? I mean, you could have told me before, but maybe..."

Flora's face darkened so rapidly that Lucas stopped in the middle of his own sentence. "There's something else," she said in a low, frightened tone.

"What?"

"A few weeks later — well, that's when I got pregnant. Around that time, that is. Chet and I only had that one time together and you and I were doing it a lot, you know, so it's not likely, but..."

Lucas' head went into a spin. He squeezed his eyes shut to avoid looking at his wife. He couldn't tell how much time had passed when he finally muttered, "Dammit," and then, "Did you ever tell Chet anything?"

"No," Flora responded in soft defiance. "What good would that have done? Chet wouldn't take care of me. You would."

LUCAS opened his eyes to find himself back on the Davis campus where he and Patton had tried to take out Royal Martin not long before. He felt fifty again — or older — and he was still looking deeply into the eyes of his wife of two decades earlier. He smiled tenderly at her, shaking his head ever so subtly.

"I never exactly apologized, did I?" Flora said ruefully.

"I never asked you to," said Lucas.

"Why not?"

"I decided it was an accident. Whose accident it was didn't seem to matter," Lucas recalled. "Life is full of accidents, after all."

"Still," Flora replied in a schoolteacherly tone, "I wish we had cleared the air a little better at the time. Things might have gone better for us afterward, you know?"

"Perhaps," Lucas replied, watching intently as his wife began to age again.

Chapter 13

"I'M AN *accident!!*" Wendy shrieked, bringing both hands down on the table with such force that silverware jostled onto the floor, her near-empty water glass tipped over on its side, spilling ice, and about a third of the people filling the Cantina restaurant turned their eyes Wendyward in shocked attention.

"Wendy?!" Cal exclaimed, half-rising from his seat as if he were prepared to leap into the day's latest emergency. But he resumed his seat when he saw a big smile blossoming on Wendy's face. She began patting the table with two hands, her dancing eyes oblivious to the stares of the other diners. *"I'm an accident, I'm an accident, I'm an..."* she kept singing happily, as if she were announcing a huge lottery prize she had just won.

Cal looked to Tom for a clue to Wendy's bizarre interruption, but he was sitting stock-still with a glaze over his eyes, his normally expressive face wearing a mask of utter neutrality. "Uh-oh," Cal mumbled to himself, turning back to Wendy to ask, "Wendy, what do you mean, you're an accident?"

Wendy let her hands rest atop the table and grinned at Cal with warmth in her voice and a glad wetness in her eyes.

"I mean, I just got it all of a sudden. About what Tom said this afternoon?"

"What Tom said?" Cal questioned wonderingly, giving the still-silent Tom a suspicious glance.

"Oh, that's right, you were off looking for Dr. Chambers," Wendy explained. "While you were gone Tom started speaking in that little voice again — the Kid, like you said? He said my parents couldn't tell me when I was really born, because my grandmother told them not to. And that I had my first birthday party twice."

"Wendy," Cal said with a look of utter confusion, "you shouldn't necessarily pay attention to everything Tom says."

"But you said the Kid was always right," Wendy reminded him.

"Well, usually, but you shouldn't start calling yourself names just because . . ."

"It's not a name," Wendy said incredulously. "It's true! I just know it is. And it explains almost everything!" Now Wendy cast her eyes Tomward, and saw that his eyes had lost the mysterious cast that, only moments before, had somehow conveyed to her the biggest single realization of her life.

After her sudden decision about breaking things off with Wayne, Wendy had realized that she was ravenously hungry and her dinner had gone untouched for nearly twenty minutes. She let Tom and Cal take over the conversation with their own concerns. Absorbed in the pleasures of eating with a new sense of freedom in her heart, she hardly paid attention to the guys until Cal started complaining about the raccoons tearing up his carefully planted garden in their Oakland back yard.

When he wondered aloud whether it was legal to procure a BB gun because then he could stay up all night and zing the little bastards when he caught them in an act of instinctual vandalism, Tom had interrupted to say, "Cal, you can't prevent every little accident," and then robotically turned to Wendy. His eyes had transformed into infinitely deep tunnels of a blazing blackness. Wendy was immediately mesmerized... some part of her mind falling, falling, falling into those tunnels, toward an unseen world of lost voices, ancient songs, and prayerful supplications. She had stopped falling when she heard one voice — unmistakably her father's — say, from a place very far away yet close enough for her to hear distinctly, "Life is full of accidents, after all." And then she had gotten it, the tunnels had closed up, and Tom's face looked merely blank to her.

"I mean, I'm just so bad at math," Wendy laughed to Cal, "that it took me all afternoon to figure it out. If I really had my first birthday twice, then my parents lied to me about when I was born. The only reason to do that is if they didn't plan to have me! And that makes sense because my mom always made such a big deal out of how much they had wanted me. Then Gramma Aggie would always come along and say, 'That's right dear, they wanted you very much.' And you know what? I never believed it!"

"Why not?" Cal asked gently, extending one hand to lay on Wendy's forearm.

"Because I always *felt* like an accident," she said. "When I was a kid, people always said *my, isn't she big for her age*, and I thought they meant I was just, you know, big! But something didn't feel right, like I didn't belong in my family. I'd look in the mirror and think I was some kind of awful mistake, just a fat little ugly girl who shouldn't be here at all."

"Oh, Wendy, now," Cal said solicitously, but Wendy raised the arm he was touching and waved him off.

"No, really, I'm okay. I mean, don't you see? If I really am an accident, I don't have to worry about whether I'm an accident! Then I can just be myself and not feel like a mistake."

Cal smiled blankly, as if he didn't really understand but was trying to be nice regardless. Wendy gestured at the crowded restaurant and tried to explain in a low, gossipy tone. "I mean, probably half the people in this place are accidents, right?"

"Almost half," Tom chimed in brightly, his demeanor back to normal.

"Oh, brother," Cal rejoined, shaking his head and turning a skeptical look toward his partner. "Tom, have you had more coffee while I wasn't looking?"

"OWWW!" Lucas cried as the inside of his skull shattered like an exploding chandelier, a thousand pieces of crystalline glass showering down through his whole body, his awareness reverberating with the violent waves of a rapidly fading blast. He sat up groggily, holding his banging head and trying to focus on his whereabouts. The last thing he could remember was looking into Flora's eyes as she took on the look she had at about age forty. He remembered feeling his greatest reluctance yet to proceed deeper into the territory of their shared past.

Then he'd heard a faint metallic creak off to his right, and whipped his head in that direction to confirm what he already knew: the turret of Patton's tank was poking through some underbrush about two hundred yards distant. The General had not left the scene after all, merely repositioned the artillery. This time the turret was pointing at Lucas and Flora dead-on, and it did not shift an iota before issuing a malevolent orange flame and a rush of smoke. Lucas had felt that he could almost read the inventory coding on the shell as it rushed toward them.

Then all was blackness.

Directly in front of him, the earth was blasted open in a pit; the shell had landed close enough to blow the married couple into the air without vaporizing them. Lucas looked around frantically for Flora, but she was nowhere to be seen. "Patton," he said grimly. He got up and began stumbling down the hill, heading toward the partially obscured tank on the opposite rise.

When he reached it he tore through the underbrush to climb up on the vehicle, where he discovered the lid open. "General, sir?" he called down into the chamber, but heard only his own metallic echo. He hopped down and stood on one of the machine's tracks, casting about to the rear for the old man. Lucas heard a shout, then the blast of a gun. There was another obscenely painful, glassy blast inside his head and he tumbled off the tank, hitting the ground with a thud, where he rolled and moaned for a few moments, clutching his scalp. When he could scramble to his feet, he broke into a run in the direction of the gunshot he'd heard.

About a hundred yards east over a small hillock, Lucas finally came upon the general in the company of a 3RD Army corpsman and a skeet-shooting apparatus. Beside the machine lay the basket of diamonds that Flora had been safekeeping, and the corpsman was loading one onto the spring-loaded launcher. Thirty feet to his left, General Patton barked, "PULL!" and one of the diamonds zinged into the air. Lucas cried out, "Wait, sir! Please wait!" Patton lowered the rifle from his shoulder and the diamond sailed on until it hit the ground in the distance.

"There you are, sonny!" Patton sang out. "I thought I'd get your attention if I shattered a few of these babies."

"Yes, sir," Lucas wheezed from his rapid run, leaning with

his hands on his knees to catch his breath. "Yes, you certainly got my attention. Where is Flora, sir? Is she all right? We were having a really important conversation before you..."

Lucas' heart sank as Patton glared at him disdainfully. "She ran off, soldier. Couldn't take the heat." Patton broke open the gun over one arm and put in two more shells from his capacious hip pocket. "And things are just beginning to heat up, sonny. But that sissy tone of voice tells me I haven't quite got your full attention yet." He nodded curtly to the corpsman, who loaded another diamond onto the launcher.

Lucas felt a flush of anger. He rushed up to the General and grabbed the gun barrel, pulling it back down to waist level. "I'm not afraid of you, sir," he said levelly, eyeing the warrior straight-on.

Patton smiled confidently and spoke in a kindly but complex tone. "Never said you should be, son. After all, I'm on your side here. You can't be running scared in a war for your own soul. But —" he added coldly, his smile fading, "you can't be consorting with the goddamn enemy anymore. We're going to need every bastard in this man's army to win the final showdown."

Lucas backed off from Patton and tilted his head, confused. "The enemy?" he asked innocently. "You mean Flora? But we're married!"

Patton snorted and stepped aggressively into Lucas' face, a sick leer contorting his features. "Married, eh? When push came to shove, that didn't make a goddamn bit of difference to her, now did it?"

AFTER Tom protested that he had not imbibed any caffeine while Cal wasn't looking — "Do you think I sneaked a coffee into the bathroom?" Tom asked sardonically — Cal sat back in his chair, arms folded, and harrumphed, "Well, there's something going on."

"Of course there's something going on," Tom replied in exasperation. "It's a heightened time, especially for Wendy. All the boundaries of awareness are more permeable than usual."

Cal looked at his partner as if he had just delivered a sentence in Greek. "I don't even want to know what that means," he replied. "When you start talking like this it just makes me nervous."

"Tom," Wendy interjected, "how much do you remember? About the voices and everything?"

"It's like my head is in a bucket," he said amiably, making the shape of a bucket with his hands up around his ears, "and the regular world is outside. I can just barely hear it, except for certain things people say. Inside the bucket, it's like I'm perfectly clear, empty. I don't hear whatever I'm saying right then, but sometimes I'll recall a bit of it later."

"So your head is in a bucket, and it's empty!" Cal laughed. "Now that I can believe."

Tom stuck his tongue out at Cal and returned to wiping sauce from his plate with two fingers as Cal smiled, stretched his arms into the air and yawned. "Well, folks, it's getting on." He lowered one arm to look at his watch. "Almost nine o'clock. I don't know about you, but I've had kind of a tiring day. What say we get back to the hotel and put in another call to the hospital? I brought my cell phone from the house, but I left it back in the room. I'll keep it with me tomorrow while we get some shopping done."

"I want some flan," Tom chirped like a nine-year-old, causing Cal to cast him a worried glance. Tom spoke again in a slowed, lower voice. "What I meant to say is, I sure would love some dessert, Dad."

"Oh, all right," Cal said. "Wendy?" he added while twisting in his chair to look for a waiter. His head stopped rotating when he was facing the restaurant entrance, and he said flatly, "Oh, for joy. It's Dr. Happy."

Just inside the restaurant foyer, standing alone before the host station, stood a white-jacketed Dr. Chambers, scratching his head and yawning. Tom looked over at him blankly, and Wendy broke out in a huge smile. Cal leaned over to his two companions and intoned, "Maybe we can pick up some goodies for you guys on the way back, okay? I'm too exhausted to deal with this character."

But Wendy had risen from her seat and started waving one arm high in the air. "Yoo-hoo, Dr. Chambers, sir!" she bellowed, drawing public attention to herself for the second time in the evening. "Come sit with us!"

Cal slumped in his chair. The doctor turned his head in surprise, then peered in the direction of Wendy's shout, pushing his glasses up the bridge of his nose. Looking left and right before moving, he trudged hesitantly to the table and stood before Cal, Wendy, and Tom as if preparing to deliver a soliloquy. He nodded curtly at Wendy and said, "Good evening, Miz Palmer. I just checked on your father before I took my break. There seems to be no alteration in his status, although he is resting safely. Sometimes there is a significant change in cases like this after the passage of the first night. If you want to check in again in the morning, I can give you a detailed progress report before I am off rotation at nine a.m." He dipped his head again and appeared ready to step away.

"Have a seat, doctor," Tom said warmly, pulling a chair from a neighboring table as Wendy nodded mutely. Cal was sitting with arms folded, regarding the physician with something less than affection.

Chambers sounded hostile as he turned his eyes to Tom. "If you **DON'T** mind, I've had an ex**HAUST**ing day and I have precious little time to myself before going back on **SHIFT**. It's very important that I con**SERVE** my energy if I am to deliver the **BEST** care to every patient on my **WATCH** — and there are **PLEN**ty of them." He sighed hugely and, facing Wendy once more, nodded to her as if to excuse himself.

Still standing, looking Chambers in the eyes across the table between them, Wendy said levelly, "I'm not afraid of you."

Cal twisted his head and looked at Wendy with surprise. Chambers took a half step backward, as if he had stumbled, and his face looked pained and vulnerable for the first time since Wendy had met him. "Why **SHOULD** you be?" he asked hollowly. "I'm just a **DOC**tor."

Chapter 14

Lucas stood before the General in shock, the movie of his worst years with Flora flickering to life in his mind. Now he was glad that she was no longer beside him. All things considered, Patton was probably a better companion to stand beside as he revisited the years when he and Flora drifted so painfully apart — drifting finally into the territory of outright betrayal. Patton was right: *when push came to shove...*

The gap between Lucas and his wife had begun to grow soon after she revealed the ancient dalliance with Chet Townsend. She claimed that telling the whole truth had lightened her heart, but Lucas felt that she had merely transferred the burden to his chest. Suddenly his youthful love affair with Flora was no longer a pure memory of delight. It was contaminated by the knowledge that Chet had scored — as Chet surely must have described it to his fratmates — with his sweetheart while Lucas was off on an innocent survey. And although Flora was probably right to believe that Chet had not sired Wendy, the doubt had been raised in Lucas' mind and wouldn't go away.

If he had been clumsy relating to his troubled daughter in her first nine years, he became utterly stiff and diffident as Wendy faced the passage out of childhood. He would sometimes forget something Wendy asked even as she stood right before him, suspiciously examining her features for signs of the Townsend genes. She was big, Chet was big; they had the same dark hair; they both had a weird, barking laugh sometimes. By the time Lucas would snap out of his moody inventory, Wendy would be biting her lip and sniffling. Then she would run off to her mother before Lucas could apologize.

Flora apparently felt so much better after telling the truth that she wanted to launch a family-wide campaign of truth-telling. She began taking herself to therapist after therapist in the evenings after her schoolteaching, suggesting often to Lucas that all three of them really should be attending the sessions together. About a year after her revelation about Chet, she had taken Lucas aside after a late dinner one evening and said, "Dr. James thinks it's time we all come in to see him and finally clear the air about Wendy. He thinks we can handle it perfectly well if we're together, in a supervised and caring environment. We just can't keep these secrets anymore, dear." Her bright voice and the enthusiastic look on her face made it sound as if she were inviting Lucas to a very special party.

Lucas grabbed Flora roughly by the arm — the closest he ever came to doing violence to her — and said, "Dear, I don't have any secrets. That's your department. We made a promise to my mother that Wendy would never know about what we had to do when she was born. That's not changing, and that's final. You're welcome to go to your therapists for the rest of your life, but please, leave me out of it."

Chastened by Lucas' unusual hostility, Flora slunk off like a kicked dog and hardly said a word about therapy for the next three or four months. After that she began talking about psychics and channelers instead. Even though she had always had an air of fantasy about her, Lucas counted this period, the turn of the decade into the 80s, as the beginning of Flora's absorption with all matters New Age.

Meanwhile Lucas' sentiments were drifting in an arguably opposite direction. In a development that felt as inevitable as it was perverse, he was becoming very big friends with Chet Townsend.

Just like the discounted car, the alliance was not Lucas' idea. Chet seemed determined to fulfill the bargain they had made for friendship, and began inviting the Palmer family out to dinner, out to movies, and over for cookouts. The first few get-togethers were forced and awkward. Flora and Monique might as well have been from different planets for all they had to share as wives and mothers — especially since Monique's son obviously preferred Flora's company. Wendy just stared at Pierre's animated play and dramatic ways of self-expression, which were generally more feminine than her own. Flora and Chet spoke to each other only in the deliberate tones of diplomacy, with Lucas listening surreptitiously for signs of intrigue.

Thus, the bond between Chet and Lucas did not begin cementing until they happened to be alone together in Chet's den on a Sunday afternoon, a little over a year since Lucas had acquired his Mercedes. After brunch at a swank hotel — the kind of thing Chet liked to do, apparently because of the chances it afforded him to run into Sacramento's up-and-coming businessmen, politicos, and their very important guests from out of town — everyone had retired to the Townsends' overfurnished ranch house to rest from the virtual frenzy of overfeeding.

Monique had excused herself with a *mal de tête* and retired to the bedroom; Wendy had retreated to the TV room with a bowl of M&Ms; Flora and Pierre had arranged all his dolls, toy cars, and a dollhouse on the dining room table as Flora led him through an abridged version of "Our Town." In the den, referred to by Chet as the "men's room" where all signs of women and children were banished, Chet laid open a box of cigars for Luke's perusal as he excitedly bustled about with his latest expensive toy, a video laser-disc player.

"I've been waiting for this for years," Chet said as he removed a record-album-sized container from a brown paper bag. "This movie really deserves to be on the big screen; a regular video just doesn't do it justice."

He beamed as he pulled the golden disc from its sleeve and slipped it into the player beneath the huge television screen. Lucas picked up the disc sleeve to find the stiff salute of George C. Scott, all done up in full military regalia, standing in front of a huge American flag. **PATTON** said the bold block lettering across the top of the sleeve, and a silver, military-style medallion in one corner added: **BEST PICTURE**, Academy Award Winner 1970. "Hey, I always wanted to see this," Lucas revealed, "but I could never get Flora to go with me when it came out. She said she didn't care about the adventures of a warmonger."

Chet harrumphed. "A warmonger who saved the Allies' ass in the Battle of the Bulge," he rumbled. "And if that wimp Eisenhower had let him take out the Russkies when he had the chance, Ron Reagan wouldn't have to be facing down the bastards today."

"Uh, yeah," Lucas added ambivalently, feeling the same unease he always felt when casual conversations verged on politics. His wife was fervently opposed to the new Republican regime in Washington, and had even gone to Berkeley with a teacher friend — dragging Wendy along — to join a protest march on the night of Reagan's election. When she returned late that night she was exhilarated, as if she'd done something that actually made a difference.

Absorbed in teaching a heavy schedule of undergraduate classes and gingerly feeling his way through campus politics at Davis, Lucas seldom found time to pay attention to such worldly concerns. There were a lot of environmental activists on the Geography faculty; they had all been bemoaning the appointment of someone named James Watt to some important government post. Lucas supposed he was against Watt, given the tide of Geography opinion. But he really needed to take the time to read some newspapers, if he ever got the chance.

"Oh, come on!" Chet interrupted Lucas' reverie by pushing the open box of cigars back at him after he had initially demurred. "You can't really watch this movie without a good Cuban. At least stick one in your mouth, Luke. You don't have to light it since you're not a smoker. These babies are getting hard to round up, let me tell you."

"Well sure, okay," Lucas conceded, taking one of the brown missiles out of its wrap and sniffing it lengthwise, just as he had seen Chet do. In his teeth, the end of the cigar tasted foul yet strangely energizing.

Chet clicked the remote smartly and Lucas' life began to change. The first time through, it was not so much the movie itself that swayed the professor, as it was Chet's utter devotion to every scene and line of dialogue. Lucas watched in wonder as Chet silently mouthed the opening prologue delivered by Patton to his troops; later, when Patton ran out of a military headquarters during an air raid by German fighter pilots, ignoring the cries of lesser officers concerned for his well-being and taking out his pistols to shoot at the planes zooming overhead, High Noon-style, Chet was out of his Barcalounger jumping for joy. "Did you see that, Luke?" Chet shouted. "Did you see? Now those were brass-plated balls on that bastard!"

Lucas had never seen a man be so passionate and uninhibited; Chet's fervor began to get to him. Watching "Patton" together became a regular thing with them, a ritual they would indulge in every few months for years. It continued well after the attempts to merge the rest of their families had run out of steam. As the 80s unfolded, the militaristic bond between Chet and Lucas was matched only by the artistic one between Flora and Pierre.

In fact, during Wendy's and Pierre's adolescent years, Lucas got used to seeing the boy around the house almost as much as his own daughter. Pierre was all of thirteen when Flora pronounced him "possessed of tremendous talent" and began borrowing him for productions staged at her high school. "He can sing, he can dance, and he has a sense of dramatic timing that's so mature for his age," she gushed. The few times that Lucas went to watch Pierre in a play, all he could see was a soft-spoken boy whose voice didn't quite reach the seats, and who moved with a gracefulness more befitting a girl than a boy.

All of which was obvious torture to Chet Townsend, whom Lucas could feel shifting uncomfortably in the hard wooden seat next to his own at every performance. Lucas had to credit his friend for his sense of duty; Chet supported his boy's dramatic tendencies through steadfast attendance, if not genuine appreciation. One Sunday afternoon not long after Pierre had turned sixteen and Flora had successfully arranged his transfer to her own high school, Chet and Lucas were chewing on Cubans in the Townsend den when the car salesman initiated a moody appraisal of the future of masculinity.

"You and me, we're a dying breed, Luke," he proclaimed in a grave tone. "My son — now there's the man of the future whether we like it or not. Sensitive, artistic, full of all those feelings that women appreciate."

"That's right," Luke affirmed, remembering all the times that Flora had prodded him to talk about his own feelings. Whatever he brought up — aggravations with fellow faculty members, frustrations with bright but inattentive students, concerns with his progress along the tenure track — always seemed to be the wrong subject. He never seemed to own the kind of feelings that Flora was after.

"I just don't know how the world is gonna keep going if it's full of faggots," Chet exclaimed bitterly.

"Hey Chet," Luke replied with alarm, "you don't really think Pierre..."

"Spare me," Chet rejoined with a sardonic shake of his leonine head, his wavy black hair just beginning to streak with gray on both sides. "I'm not an idiot, Luke. And I don't hate faggots, I just can't understand how —" he paused to look up through the skylight and sighed. "D'you know what happened when I tried to tell Pierre about sex? Give him the old father-to-son talk, I mean?"

"No," Lucas said softly, wondering if Flora had given Wendy any sort of talk by now.

"I didn't get ten words out of my mouth before he says, 'Oh Dad, we've already had that AIDS education thing at school' and then he tells me he's got to practice his lines. End of story! And that's not even the worst of it."

"It isn't?"

"Get this, Luke. Couple days later Monique comes up and asks me what the word 'antediluvian' means. I ask her why and she says, 'Pierre has told me you tried to give him an *antediluvian* lecture about le sex. Quest-ce que c'est?' Jesus, I had to look it up. So my son thinks I'm a goddamn dinosaur."

"Well, Chet," Lucas responded firmly, suppressing a grin owing to the gravity of the situation, "you're just traditional. There's nothing wrong with that. God knows I'd appreciate a little more tradition in my own household."

"Oh yeah? How's that?" Chet asked, leaning back in his easy chair, his face brightening a little.

"It's Flora. I can't keep up with all her New Age fads. She's always chattering about this psychic or that guru, and she has so many wild ideas flying around in her head I wonder how she keeps track of them. I mean, if it's Tuesday it must be Wicca, if it's Thursday it must be the course in goddamn *miracles*." Lucas spit off the last few words with a real bitterness, impressing himself with how tough he sounded.

Chet pulled his cigar from his mouth, regarding his pal with a look of total incomprehension. "Sounds tough, buddy. The things we men have to put up with these days."

LUCAS felt a coarse kick to his rump and looked up to see Patton towering over him. Without realizing it, Lucas had sunk to the ground in a cross-legged squat during his latest reverie. His introspection had been so deep that he had not noticed a most remarkable development around him: the massing of an army. As far as Lucas could see across the flatlands surrounding Davis, thousands of uniformed men and gray-green machines of war were arranging themselves into traveling formations, churning up billowing clouds of dust. Lucas scrambled to his feet in amazement. "Sir?" he asked haplessly.

"Well, are you going with us to the front, soldier, or are you going to sit here and wallow in nostalgia?"

"The front, sir? What front? Where are we headed?"

"About-face, sonny. The big battle is back the way we came."

"You mean, back in the real world?" Lucas asked hopefully, remembering the idyllic landscape where he and Flora had been sitting so peacefully before Patton's first tank attack.

"Nope," Patton replied, slipping on his helmet and straightening his uniform. "Sacramento." He waved his left arm in a broad gesture and the entire 3RD Army revved its engines, creating a magnificent rumble across the land. "Our intelligence reports that the enemy is holed up in your mother's house in the capital city," he shouted above the din. "We're going to dislodge her from that stronghold, or we'll all die trying!"

"Of course, sir," Lucas said absent-mindedly. He had not heard the General's last statement because a nagging question had arisen from his memories. "Sir, is it all right if I catch a ride with the rear guard? I have some, uh, personal matters to clear up before I can join the fray and be at my best."

Patton eyed Lucas testily, flicking his short whip against his baggy leggings. "All right, soldier," he finally relented, "take five. But don't lollygag too long. I'll need you on the front when push comes to shove. And don't get run over, sonny!"

Lucas hopped backward just in time to avoid being crushed by an onrushing line of personnel carriers. Roaring with laughter, Patton leapt onto the back of one of the trucks loaded with soldiers, who all rose in a cheer as they pulled him on board. Lucas waved half-heartedly to the troops racing by as he clumsily stepped backward until he found a tree trunk to sit down against. He began sinking rapidly into the past again — back into the 1980s when Flora was flaking out, Pierre was developing his stagecraft, Chet was making a small fortune at the dealership, and he, Professor Palmer, was beginning to solidify his academic reputation.

But what about Wendy? Lucas was asking himself in a near-panic. *Where was Wendy? What did we do with Wendy?* For the life of him, he couldn't remember raising his own daughter anymore.

Chapter 15

WENDY was dreaming a most agreeable dream. The familiar smell of the dusty African plain filled her nostrils as she rocked herself sensually to the insistent rhythm of the ritual drums pounding away on all sides of her. She was at the head of a circle of tribal leaders, none quite so powerful as herself, yet each important enough to be reckoned with. She cast her eyes around the array of colorful robes and signifying headwraps and, with a slight nod of her head, acknowledged the key leaders of influence in the circle: Yaphet Kotto, James Earl Jones, Ving Rhames, and that most heavily bejeweled and dangerous buffoon, Mr. T. At one time or another every one of these men had raised challenges to her territorial regime. And each had paid dearly in the blood of their tribesmen.

Now she had gathered them all to meet the new emblem of her power, the magical factor that would guarantee the eminence of her reign forever: her medicine man from the future. She snapped her fingers and the circle broke open to admit Dr. Chambers, striding toward her in his white jacket, a stethoscope dangling from his neck. As he approached, Wendy pulled down roughly on her robe, exposing one chocolate-brown, magnificently massive breast tipped with a blue-black nipple. All the men in the circle gasped except the physician, who stepped forward confidently to apply his scope to Wendy's exposed upper chest. He listened intently for a moment, then dropped the instrument to give Wendy a confident double-thumbs-up sign. The crowd roared in acclamation as Dr. Chambers bent tenderly over Wendy's face to bring his lips to meet her own...

Wendy woke with a moan, her lips pouting helplessly toward the missing Dr. Chambers, and then sighed. "I never get kissed," she mumbled sleepily, then yawned and turned her face to look at the radio clock beside the hotel bed. Nine o'clock. She sat up abruptly, first remembering that Dr. Chambers had said his shift was over at nine. Then she recalled with a guilty chill that her father could be dead by now. She leapt from the bed in her bra and panties from the day before, rapidly unwrapped the new white shirt that Cal had brought from Guerneville, and threw it on herself while rushing toward the door, breathlessly trying to clasp the buttons.

Outside the neighboring room she stopped fumbling with the buttons long enough to pound on the door and issue a muffled shout: "Cal! Tom! Are you awake? Maybe we should get going to the hospital?"

Silence answered her; she pounded the door once more. Finally she heard Tom's sleepy voice responding: "Uh, yeah, Wendy? Just a minute, I'm not decent. Cal went down to the lobby, I think. Just a sec..."

"Never mind," Wendy barked, and rushed to the elevator, finishing the shirt buttons just as the door swished open. She scrambled inside, pounded the Lobby button and found herself hopping in place as the metal box laboriously made its way to the bottom. As soon as the doors began to open she jumped through them, colliding with Cal.

"Whoa there, Wendy!" he laughed, aggressively pushing her back into the elevator. "For Chrissakes girl, you don't have any pants on!"

"Oh my God," Wendy gasped. "Have you called Dr. Chambers? Is my father okay? I slept too long!"

"Hey, calm down," Cal said reassuringly, patting Wendy on the shoulder before punching an elevator button. "I called in about an hour ago and spoke to Dr. Happy personally. He said there's no change, nothing to worry about. We can check in later when the ward is open, around lunch time. I thought I'd let you get some rest while I read the paper. If there was anything serious happening, I'd have let you know."

"Thank God," Wendy said with a collapsing sigh, embarrassed for the first time by her half-nakedness. As the elevator doors opened on their floor, both she and Cal peeked out into the hallway in different directions. Then Cal gave Wendy a push, chuckling, "Go for it!"

"But I left my key-card thingie in the room!" she exclaimed. "That was stupid."

Cal produced a spare from his shirt pocket. "I got an extra for your room, just in case." They walked to her door and Cal slipped the card in, opened the door, and stood aside to let Wendy go in. He held open the door an extra moment and spoke quietly. "Uh, Wendy, I guess I should tell you. Dr. Chambers actually said that the fact there's been no change *is* something to worry about. Some of your dad's vital signs are not great. But there's nothing to do except wait, and there isn't anything we can do there. They won't let us in the ICU til noon. I'll keep in touch by cell phone this morning, and any time you want to go, we'll go, okay?"

"Okay," Wendy said quietly. "Thanks, Cal. I'm gonna get dressed the rest of the way now." As the door closed on Cal, Wendy somberly stepped over to the corner of the bed where she had tossed her stretchy black slacks from the night before. She gathered them in her hands and turned to face the mirror over the low dresser. Now she regretted that she had nothing else to wear — not just in the hotel room, but back home in Sacramento as well. Except for the sake of keeping herself clean, Wendy had hardly changed what she wore for years, and the realization made her inexpressibly sad. That was strange because until this moment, the sameness of her wardrobe had always made her feel safe, even a little superior.

She didn't need to dress up in a feminine fashion like other women, she had always told herself. She was above advertising her body or getting herself noticed by strange men on the street. Who needed all the seeking, resistance, and deception that went on in games of flirtation? Why couldn't people be appreciated just for what they were inside, regardless of their physical appearance? For Wendy it had long been sufficient to slip on one of her father's white shirts — even though they had begun to be a little tight across her chest and belly in the last few years — and wear it untucked, like a tent concealing everything that existed beneath her neck. Her reason for wearing black pants was less clear to her, if more emotionally charged — it just seemed safest to paint everything down there with darkness. Her uniform was plain but honest, Wendy had always told herself — *what you see is all you get*, she would even boast occasionally.

All of which now felt like a cowardly lie, Wendy realized as she gazed in the mirror at her frazzled hair, her shirt, and her exposed, lumpy legs. An ancient venom for herself that she often felt in front of mirrors was rising again. Wendy was doubly depressed to feel its return when she had felt so high the night before. Even though she hadn't been able to make Cal understand why recognizing her accidentalness was so liberating, the insight had given her the impulsive courage to confront Dr. Chambers.

Thereafter the physician had mumbled a vague apology, dropped himself heavily into the chair Tom had offered, and spent ten minutes spilling out complaints about his job — how he was always too rushed to provide the kind of quality care he meant to provide, how black doctors, especially young brilliant ones, were discriminated against, and so on. Wendy had listened avidly, even though many of Dr. Chambers' troubles were familiar to her from episodes of "ER" and "Chicago Hope." She couldn't say that she and the doctor had exactly bonded; he spoke in a monologue that ended only when Cal brusquely announced that they needed to leave in order for Wendy to get her rest. Still, she had gone to bed feeling powerful and full of hope, and then she had awakened with that dream...

There was a sharp rap at her door and Wendy jumped, realizing that she didn't know how much time had passed as she stood in front of the mirror, clutching her pants. "Ready in ten!" Cal proclaimed cheerily from behind the door. She nearly yelled back *Leave me alone!* before recalling that Cal was planning to take her shopping as long as her dad remained alive. The prospect was both fearful and tantalizing. She wondered for a moment about the comparative time spans of typical comas vs. your everyday shopping expedition. Then she hurried into her pants and flat shoes.

The five-story hotel that Cal had found for them was a few

blocks from downtown Santa Rosa, a pleasant walk on another day that had dawned comfortably warm and glorious, just like the momentous day before. Wendy's spirits began lifting again as the trio ambled into the languid luxury of a Sonoma Sunday morning, with Tom fussing about his state of near-starvation owing to a missed dessert from the night before.

Wendy was a little hungry herself, but she noted with curiosity that the hunger was delightfully simple: she was hungry, she would eat something, and that would be that. Before this morning, a feeling of hunger (or anything passing for it) had always been the occasion for drawing up an inner battle plan for seeking out healthy food, avoiding unhealthy food, and concealing the total volume of whatever she ate from whomever might be watching. *Why is everything different today?* she wondered, and mumbled without thinking, "My dad can't be dying every day."

"What was that, Wendy?" Cal said, leaning over to hear her as they turned a corner in the central part of town.

"Oh, nothing," she hastily demurred, then pointed diagonally across the intersection and said, "Oh goody! There's a Starbucks next to that Barnes & Noble!" She knew the territory well in both franchises.

But she felt Cal's arm go around her shoulder and start steering her to the other side of the street, where a sign advertised a café adjoining another bookstore named Copperfields. "Where are we going?" she asked in confusion.

Tom laughed caustically and said, "Wendy, you bad girl! We don't go to chain stores." Wendy gave Tom a puzzled look and he lifted his eyebrows toward Cal on her other side. "If my boyfriend has a religion, it has something to do with independent bookstores and neighborhood coffeehouses," he explained. "He gets a little rigid sometimes, if you know what I mean." Then he added impishly, "Although I could tolerate a little more rigidity under the right circumstances."

Cal broke from his half-embrace of Wendy to duck behind her and kick Tom in the ass, who then turned about and started slapping at his boyfriend until they were both jumping and dodging each other on the sidewalk, cackling loudly and drawing the attention of the Starbucks customers sitting outside in the mid-morning sun. Wendy placed her hands on her hips, feeling an irrepressible grin spreading across her face. She proclaimed harshly, "Now boys, if you don't behave, nobody gets any breakfast. Except me, that is."

Tom bowed his head and said, "Sorry, mom. I'll be good," and Cal laughed while pushing open the door to the Copperfields café. After the three had gotten some pastries and coffee — in Tom's case, herbal tea — and taken seats at a table by the window, Cal began looking at a small ring-binder notepad he produced from his shirt pocket. He was holding it beneath the table, trying not to look obvious while Tom and Wendy chatted about bookstores. Cal's absorption finally drew Wendy's attention. When she asked what he was looking at, Cal looked uncomfortable and said it was nothing, folding the note-book shut and slipping it back in his pocket.

"Oh, I bet," Tom chirped, deftly plucking the pad from Cal's shirt, flipping it open and starting to read aloud while tilting Cal's writing toward Wendy's view. "One summer dress, pantsuit (maybe), two pair shoes, stockings (question mark), new foundations... *foundations*?" Tom giggled, looking at his partner in disbelief. "What decade are you living in?"

Wendy was staring at Cal as well. "Cal, what is this? I can't afford all this stuff!"

Looking unusually nervous, Cal snatched the notebook back from Tom and said sternly, "Wendy, you need some new clothes. I think you'll feel better about yourself, considering everything you have to deal with right now, and in the days to come." He paused, looking found out, and then regained his normal confidence. "It's the least Tom and I can do for you in this, um, heightened time. Consider it our little present."

Wendy turned back to Tom, who grinned and said, "Congratulations, Wendy. You've just become a Calvin Davidson Project." But he was looking at her with genuine warmth. She reached slowly for the notebook and Cal let it go without resistance. Peering at the list again, Wendy asked a question in a tone of voice that betrayed equal parts of awe and suspicion:

"Why are you guys taking care of me?"

SLUMPED against a tree trunk while Patton's 3RD Army continued to rumble by him on its advance toward Sacramento, Lucas wondered in shame why his recent inventory of the past revealed so few memories of Wendy's upbringing. He suddenly recalled a summery Saturday morning in the mid-1980s, when Wendy would have been about — fifteen? (sixteen)? He was walking into the sunny kitchen nook where Flora always liked to do her reading. He spied a blue book laid open to a page that said "Step Four: Made a searching and fearless moral inventory of ourselves."

"What's this, honey?" he asked amiably of Flora, who was in the kitchen making French toast for the two of them. The house felt relaxed and quiet, mostly because Wendy was away for a few weeks at a weight-control camp. Lucas and Flora were both convinced of the usefulness of various summer camps and other organized, socialized approaches to resolving Wendy's problems. Although she never came back any different, Lucas was always secretly grateful that Wendy's tantrums and crying jags were removed from the house for weeks at a time. At fifteen, she could be a holy terror.

Flora bent down to look through the gap between the kitchen counter and the stove hood, and said neutrally, "Oh, I'm reading up on the Twelve Steps program, dear. You know, Alcoholics Anonymous?"

Lucas closed the book and flipped it from front to back a few times. He asked soberly, "Are you a drunk, Flo?"

Something clattered to the floor in the kitchen and Flora soon came around the dividing wall, holding the pan of French toast in one hand and an oven mitt in the other. Her face displayed a wide-eyed look of utter hilarity. "Luke, I sweah," she said in an eruption of the native accent that was otherwise wearing away in the West Coast milieu, "sometimes your elevatuh just don't make it to the penthouse." She was laughing as she set the oven mitt on the table and the pan of still-sizzling wedges of bread on top of it. "If I were drinking I think you'd know about it, dear. But you know, we all get a little drunk on something."

"We do?" Lucas asked curiously as he took his seat, gratefully eyeing the breakfast before him. "Like what?"

"Well," Flora mused as she leaned on one of the chairs with both hands, "I get a little drunk on the theatah, you know. Not that that's a bad thing. And you can still get drunk poring over those maps of yours. Why, on our first date you tried to get me drunk on them. Most boys would have used beer, you know." Flora was grinning seductively, and Lucas blushed. "Or take somebody like Chet Townsend — now he gets drunk on all that expensive junk he buys. Not to mention certain bloodthirsty war heroes," she added with a knowing grin.

Lucas refused the bait, picking up the book again to stare at the spine. Then he gazed at his wife blankly. "No, really. Why are you reading this stuff?"

Flora drew back her chair and sat down with a sigh. "Dear, in case you hadn't noticed, our daughter has a food addiction. That's why we sent her to camp, remember?"

"Wendy?" Lucas asked in disbelief. "Oh, she's a little heavy, that's all. The school psychologist said it was just a problem of impulse control, didn't he?"

"Same thing, dear," Flora said didactically. "Anyway, Lanier says we have to look deeper than that. She says that addictive patterns are rooted in the family system. Maybe even deeper than that — like in our karma?" By the last word, Flora's voice had weakened almost to a whisper. She pushed back her chair and stood, saying nervously, "I forgot the spatula."

Lucas took a deep breath and picked up his fork to snag two pieces of the French toast. Lanier was a new sore spot between Lucas and Flora; he had recently adopted a policy of changing the subject whenever Flora dropped the name of her latest therapeutic confidant. He understood the attraction of Lanier being a fellow Southerner, and at least the woman had earned a counseling degree. But she had also developed a sideline of going into trances to speak in the clumsy Irish brogue of someone who claimed to be both wise and long-dead. Flora had once subjected him to an audience with Lanier and her "source," and he had hardly been able to contain his derision. His mirthful silence said enough, he trusted.

At least the scene had served as a juicy little chestnut to tell Chet Townsend at their next tête-à-tête: Chet was incredulous, saying "Oh no, man, you've got to be kidding" and "How do you put up with this bullshit?" and "Well, you're a more patient man than I am, Professor Palmer."

By the time Flora returned to the dining table, spatula in hand and a tentative, hopeful smile on her face, Lucas had his mouth full of bread and syrup. He could sincerely say, "This is great, Flo," and segue to safer subject matter. By ignoring the annoyance called Lanier, he had also dismissed, once again, the problem named Wendy.

Chapter 16

"DESTINY?" Cal replied in answer to Wendy's inquiry about why he and Tom were so solicitous toward someone they had met less than twenty-fours before. No one challenged him so he confirmed his own guess in a matter-of-fact tone: "Destiny."

"There's no escaping destiny," Tom chimed in.

Wendy's eyes widened. "That's so weird!" she exclaimed. "I mean, my mom used to say that all the time — especially after she got sick." Wendy's face fell and she began pushing a half-eaten croissant around on its plate.

"She was the redhead in that picture, right?" Cal ventured. "Real beautiful lady. I thought she looked like some kind of movie star."

Wendy looked up again, smiling nostalgically. "She would have loved to hear you say that. She was an actress and a director and a playwright, you know."

"Really?" Cal responded, seeming genuinely interested. "Did she do anything we would know about?"

"Oh no," Wendy demurred, "just local stuff in Sacramento. She taught drama in high school. I guess she had wanted to go to Broadway when she was young, but she and Dad got married so early — and now I know the real reason why," she added with a quick rise and drop of her shoulders.

"You loved your mother," Tom stated flatly.

Wendy nodded her head, biting her lip. "Yeah. We were closer than me and my dad. Sometimes he acted like he hardly knew who I was, until the last few years when he was falling all over himself trying to help me…" Wendy stopped cold, suddenly aware that she was already speaking of her father in the past tense. She wondered if Tom and Cal were noticing, but was afraid to look either of them in the eyes. "I mean, he's really sweet in his own way. He tries, he just doesn't know what to do with me."

"So you've been staying in the same house together since your mother…?" Cal inquired softly.

"Yes, about three years now since she died. It was breast cancer. She went really quickly after they found it — less than a year. I don't think my father is over it yet, or if he ever will be. Especially the last few months he's seemed kind of frozen. I don't mean quiet, cause he's always been quiet. He actually moves real slow, like he's getting arthritis or something. But I can't ever ask him how he's doing — he just says, 'don't worry about me, little girl, you have enough to worry about.' Like I need to be reminded?" She sighed and added meanly, "Or like I'm still little, or ever was?" Impulsively she grabbed the remains of the croissant, and stuffed it in her mouth all at once.

"O-kay," Cal intervened with a businesslike enunciation, "I think it's time we get this show on the road. I'm going to give the hospital a call, and then let's walk down to that shopping center we passed. It's no Union Square, but it'll have to do." He pushed back his chair, stretched, and surreptitiously nodded to Tom to indicate that he should somehow distract Wendy, who was now staring longingly at the pastry shelves across the room. But then he reached out to touch her hand himself. "By the way Wendy, this morning I left a message at Townsend Mercedes in Sacramento about the situation here. I suppose Mr. Townsend will get it pretty soon. Most car dealers are open on Sunday."

Wendy gave no reply, simply standing in place next to where she had been sitting, seemingly waiting to be led away. Tom and Cal exchanged worried glances over her rapid change of demeanor, then each of them took one of her arms to guide her back out to the sidewalk. They had traversed no more than half a block before they came upon a small storefront window painted with pink script, announcing *Bernard's Beauty & Hair*. As they came abreast of the shop, the door opened and a delicate, balding man of about fifty-five in a fine silk vest and well-tailored slacks emerged from within to shade his eyes and look at the sun, finding three strangers in his light instead. He quickly scanned Cal and Tom and merrily chirped, "Why hello there! Out-of-towners, I'll bet!"

"Destiny," Tom whispered weirdly, apparently speaking to no one visible.

Cal placed one arm around Wendy's shoulders and pushed her toward the shopkeeper with his other hand. He nodded toward Wendy's hair and said, "We're kind of in a hurry today. What can you do in an hour?"

Bernard stepped back and tilted his head one way and then the other, sizing up Wendy — who was just coming out of her moody glaze to look back and forth between the three men in confusion. "Well, we can do a cut and a little shaping, I guess… sure, we can do something nice. You're lucky cause I'm not usually in on Sunday, but I've got a special coming in about an hour. So everything will work out, hey? You guys gonna stick around?" he asked eagerly.

"No, I'm afraid we've gotta survey the territory ahead," Cal demurred. "What do you recommend for women's fashions around here? You know, for. . ." He nodded sideways toward Wendy again.

"Oh, well," Bernard said, obviously crestfallen, "I don't know exactly. I haven't bought anything for myself since a little frock last Halloween!" He laughed without getting a significant response, then soberly pointed down the street. "I guess you can just try Macy's there in the Plaza. As good a place as any." Bernard took Wendy's hand and said warmly, "So what do you feel like today, Miss…?"

"Wendy. Nothing too radical," Wendy blurted anxiously, twisting about to look back toward Cal and Tom as Bernard led her to a styling chair. Her unexpected companions of the weekend waved back at her, and Cal raised his cell phone to mime the call he was about to make.

"Honey, this is Santa Rosa," Bernard said sardonically. "We never get radical here."

LUCAS pushed himself up from his seat by the tree trunk and flagged down an oncoming Jeep, grumbling about a waste of time. He was angry at himself now for not taking the ride that Patton had offered earlier, especially since his latest review of the past had netted him only sorrow and self-flagellation over his role as Wendy's father. Once again Patton had been proven right: men of action didn't waste time on "searching moral inventories." Now he might miss the battle raging at the front, and he had no one but himself to blame.

The dirty green Jeep chucked to a stop in front of Lucas and its fresh-faced driver hopped out smartly, drawing himself up ramrod-straight to salute the professor. "Dr. Palmer, sir!" he barked, but Lucas waved him down as he hopped into the passenger's seat. "As you were, sonny," he replied, tossing off his own casual salute. "Just get me to the front as quick as you can. I've got to be there when push comes to shove." The young corpsman beamed mightily, replying "Yes, sir!" and began laying on the horn as the Jeep lurched forward. "Out of the way there!" the driver shouted as he zoomed around a puttering troop carrier full of sleepy-eyed grunts. "Out of the way! I've got the *Professor* here!"

Bouncing roughly in his thinly padded seat, Lucas turned his head to give his attaché a supportive smile and thought to himself, *Now there's a promising young man. The kind of boy Chet Townsend would have been proud to call his own...* but the very word *Townsend* suddenly rankled him. Lucas began to feel a vindictive zeal for battle rising in his blood.

The whole problem had been the close ties to the Townsends, Lucas thought bitterly, and that had never been his idea. Chet had suckered him with that damn Mercedes; from there on the Palmers and the Townsends had grown ever more entwined. By the time Wendy was a senior in high school — barely making good enough grades to ensure her graduation but revealing no prospects for life thereafter — Flora had practically adopted Pierre. He actually spent two or three nights a week in one of the Palmers' extra rooms, owing to all the late rehearsals that he and Flora were attending at the high school and with her fledgling dramatic troupe, the Bright Lights Theatre Company. More than once Lucas drove home from a late University Senate meeting in Davis to find an impromptu cast party going on in his kitchen, populated by his wife, Pierre and his special friend Romero, and an assorted cast of excitable, flamboyant young characters that Lucas could hardly believe existed in the environs of Sacramento.

This was the same period, the late 1980s, when Flora had begun her embarrassing career as a playwright — a development that tried Lucas' charity in more ways than one. For the first time in their lives together Flora began "borrowing" money from him to keep the company alive until they had their first big hit and outside investors would, of course, start calling. But the cash flow was less of a burden than having to hear readings and watch weekend rehearsals for Flora's dramatic compositions, which were uniformly mawkish and awkwardly metaphysical — peopled with winged angels and veiled seers, modern witches and ancient archetypes, weeping heroines and muscular dragon-slayers. Perhaps because she surrounded herself with high school and junior-college talent, Flora never seemed to catch onto her weaknesses as a dramatist. She defiantly continued her community theatre experiments in the face of paltry audiences, snide or nonexistent reviews from the local press, and her husband's ambivalence.

One evening when Lucas had decided he should spend some quality time with his daughter and found himself sitting silently with her in the TV room, dully watching the long string of sitcoms and medical dramas that largely occupied Wendy's consciousness, Flora entered to ask his opinion of the new play she had nearly finished. She excitedly described a plot that involved an angel deciding to drop his wings in order to pursue an earth-bound love affair. Lucas had to bite his tongue to keep from pointing out that even he, a culturally retarded geography professor, recognized this to be one of the most hackneyed plots of dramatic literature. Instead he just nodded and smiled occasionally, enough to keep Flora talking while he tried to keep up with the absurd antics of a Seinfeld episode. The show left him cold but seemed to keep his daughter giggling — a rare expression he'd surely lost the knack for inducing over the years.

Finally Flora had gotten to the point. "So my title is," she said with the breathless anticipation of an Academy Award presenter, '*Where Angels Fear to Shed*.' What do you think, honey? Does that hit you right? Can you just not wait to see it, I mean?"

Lucas started in his seat on the sofa with the violent reaction of a man about to laugh out loud and holding in his hilarity by force. He wanted to say, *It sounds utterly vacuous*, but that seemed unnecessarily cruel. He vented his suppressed laughter with the most caring smile he could manage and commented, "Well, it's awfully clever, Flo, but are you sure people will take it seriously? They might think you're just trying to make a joke, and the play sounds so, ahh — *tragic*."

"Oh, really?" Flora said with bright-eyed concern, penciling a note on her loose sheaf of papers. "Oh dear, I hadn't thought of that. Thank you so much, honey." Then she retired to the kitchen nook, her habitual writing studio, just as a gangly clown called Kramer took a pratfall on the tube and Wendy started barking with weird, Chetlike laughter. Later that night Flora would thank Lucas profusely in bed for his brilliant insight, leading to one of the rarely satisfying episodes of their sporadic sex life.

All of which might have been bearable — it was not the worst life to lead, after all — had not Chet Townsend starting leaning hard on Lucas for an entirely different kind of insight. After a decade of friendship, Lucas had become accustomed to Chet's signature ebullience being punctuated by fits of self-pity. But

Lucas had never heard his friend sound so blue as the morning in February 1989 when Chet unexpectedly called him to meet for breakfast. Chet's tone was so down, in fact, that Lucas accepted the invitation without question. That necessitated a phone call to a sleepy teaching assistant in Davis to ask him to take over the professor's morning classes.

Lucas caught up with a red-eyed Chet at a coffee shop near the Capitol building. The professor had no sooner slid into the booth, motioning to a waitress for a menu, than the car salesman blurted out what was on his mind.

"She's gone, Luke."

"Gone? Who's gone?"

"Monique. She left me. Came back from the dealers' conference in L.A. a few days late, and she had just cleared out everything."

"No, Chet," Luke responded with a hollow whisper, truly aghast.

"Yeah," the beefy man sighed. "Left a 'dear Chet' note all in goddamn French, just to spite me. Took me about an hour to figure it out. She said she never belonged here and was going back to her family to find herself."

Lucas reached over to grasp Chet's wrist and give it a reassuring squeeze. "Well, Chet, I'm sure it's just a temporary thing. She just needs a little time away from home."

"Her family's in goddamn *Nice*, Luke. She took everything she owned, and about a dozen things of mine, all the way to France. She won't be back. Left her attorney's card with the note. I didn't even know she had a goddamn attorney of her own."

Lucas withdrew his hand and whistled softly to cover his speechlessness. The waitress appeared and Lucas absentmindedly ordered a breakfast while Chet shoved his cup to the edge of the table and said, "Just more coffee." After he got his refill and the young woman returned to the kitchen, Chet eyed Lucas morosely and mumbled, "Maybe I shouldna been fuckin' Doreen."

"What?!" Lucas choked, his mind's eye instantaneously stripping the super-buxom twenty-something he had seen a few times typing up sales contracts outside Chet's office.

"Yeah," Chet responded with a look that passed for thoughtfulness. "I didn't tell you before, because, you know, you're a pretty straight and narrow guy and — not that I think you would tell anyone, it's just with Flora and Pierre being so tight — anyway, Doreen is why I got back late from the dealers' conference. She just had to see Disneyland, at her age! So there I was spinning around in a damn teacup while my wife is packing up the place."

Lucas couldn't help himself; his next question just popped out. "Doreen, huh? So, how is she anyway?"

Chet smiled for the first time in their meeting. "Well, if you ever wondered what it was like to nail Dolly Parton — but all-natural, if you know what I mean..."

Thus began a new and dubious phase of male bonding between the salesman and professor. Chet's grief over Monique's abandonment lasted all of two weeks, rapidly supplanted by his righteous aggravation over divorce proceedings and the exhilaration of a rambunctious, frequently irresponsible midlife dating spree. Chet often wanted to discuss his conquests with Lucas, seeking moral counsel that largely went ignored in the heat of his next flirtation or betrayal. At first Lucas was honored to be consulted, but after a while the indulgence of so much vicarious sexuality began to rankle him. Especially since Chet considered him such a "straight and narrow" guy.

All the more so because it was undeniably true. The closest Lucas had ever come to an affair was his truncated flirtation with Viola, the brilliant, willowy graduate student who had inspired him to run for the University Senate's Planning Council. That political plum would have cinched his tenure and put him on the same power track as his retired mentor, Dr. Royal Martin. But after a few months of campaigning and glad-handing at various campus social functions, Lucas proved to have no instinct for the political jugular. He would get his tenure appointment soon enough anyway, having published just enough ploddingly safe papers in the right insular journals to establish himself as another undistinguished twinkle in the academic firmament.

But the night of the campus vote — the same Thursday night that Flora was debuting her musical "My Life as Cleopatra" back in Sacramento — became an acutely bittersweet memory for Lucas. After the votes had been counted and he came up short, he took Viola's soft, graceful hand amidst the falling balloons and spilled plastic cups of punch in a crowded conference room and said, "Oh well, Viola, that's the way the cookie crumbles. Thank you for working so hard for me. I wouldn't even have tried for it without you."

Without warning Viola had pulled her favorite instructor close to herself and whispered in his ear, "I have a place we can go tonight, Professor." Her tone was seductive, dead serious. So the weeks of signals, suggestive joking, and sweet smiles that had gone on between them during the campaign were not just a product of Lucas' imagination; this beautiful, ambitious, and incredibly collected young woman actually wanted him.

And he would have gone along with his wave of desire — risking scandal, dishonor, even the possible loss of his career

— had it not been for a sobering realization at the moment of decision. At that moment, looking deep into Viola's searching and excited eyes, he had realized that she was not the perfect mistress, a compensation for imperfect wifely love at home. No, Viola was another kind of substitute; she was the perfect daughter that had been denied him.

So Lucas had smiled sadly and said firmly, "I'm sorry, Viola. You're a lovely young woman with quite a future ahead of you, and I think you know that I find you very attractive. But this is the moment at which I'm supposed to say no, for both our sakes. Especially for yours. And that's what I'm saying: No. I'm very sorry."

Noble, but hardly the kind of story I could boast about to Chet, Lucas mused as he vibrated in the shockless Jeep careening toward the front. Or to anyone else. His longing to rejoin Patton and feel the heat of the final battle was intensifying as the 3RD Army gained speed on Interstate 80 heading east. The hulking gray-green conveyances of the warriors had commandeered the highway so completely that ordinary traffic had been shunted to the shoulders in a scattered array of cursing carpoolers and snorting tractor-trailers. Lucas smiled and waved condescendingly at all the civilians leaning against their fenders, anxiously checking their watches and gesturing helplessly at the military caravan roaring past them.

Then he stood up in front of his seat, holding onto the metal frame of the flimsy windshield to peer ahead at the distant, low skyline of Sacramento. He was fervently hoping that Patton did not vanquish the enemy in one brilliant strategic stroke before he could get in a few volleys of fire himself. For as he returned to his seat, giving his young driver a paternal punch on the shoulder, he could feel his long-controlled anger mounting toward an explosive peak — just as his memories took another dark, unwanted, yet irresistible turn.

His family's emotional entanglements with the Townsends had come to a head when Lucas found himself in the middle of a power struggle over the future of Pierre Townsend. He supposed that Flora got so involved because it was probably too depressing to think about her own daughter's destiny. After high school no one could quite figure out what to do with Wendy; she seemed content to stay at the house and watch TV for the rest of her life. Lucas was already feeling so guilty about being a poor father that he didn't have the gumption to push her out of the nest. He knew she would fall heavily, and the ground was a long way down.

Flora, always the more inventive parent, started using the excuse that Wendy was helpful to have around to run show-related errands. That was only half-true since Wendy had a tendency to forget what she was doing half the time, sitting moodily in coffee shops or a busy mall for an hour or two when she was supposed to be picking up costumes or printed programs. One evening Lucas came home to find the seldom-used formal dining room filled to the brim with printed recipes and boxes of envelopes; Flora had found Wendy an at-home job stuffing envelopes for a mail-order company. Lucas just shook his head at the mess that night. The next morning he offered his daughter falsely enthusiastic congratulations on her new employ.

To say the least, Wendy's future did not shine with promise. But Flora had become convinced that Pierre was going to be the next bright star on Broadway. She was lending sympathy and vocal support to the boy's plan to move to New York with his boyfriend Romero and start trying out for positions in the leading modern dance companies. Pierre had already faced down his father over Chet's insistence that he go to junior college and get a business administration degree before he tested his talents in New York. But he was smart enough to know he needed money to give him a year or two's head start, or become mired in restaurant jobs while his lithe, youthful frame wasted away.

"These are his prime years to learn from the great teachers," Flora would say to Lucas. "He just needs a little boost to get on his feet. Is that really too much to ask from his dad?"

Lucas heard that side of the story at home, and the other side from an aggrieved Chet at their now-weekly breakfast meetings near the Capitol. "It's like living with a total stranger," Chet complained one morning about the cold war raging between himself and his son, almost two years after Pierre had graduated from high school. "He just comes and goes with that damn boyfriend of his and hardly speaks a word. I know he's trying to make it so unpleasant that I'll give him the money just to get rid of him. But I'll be damned if I'm going to give him and that little Cuban fag the funds to set up housekeeping in New York and go to auditions all day. The boy's got to get some sense in his head, stop living for all these wild dreams." Chet sighed heavily, then raised his hands in a gesture of helpless incredulity. "Boy thinks he's gonna be the next Fred Astaire, for God's sake!"

"Or Merce Cunningham," Luke corrected, remembering a name bandied about in the Palmer household.

"Yeah, whoever," Chet huffed. "Luke, I hate to lean on you like this, but maybe you could ask Flora to talk some sense into Pierre? She's been a big influence on him, and I'm sure he'd listen to her. I'm not saying he can't be a star someday, but you and I know you can't put all your eggs in one basket. I mean, am I right?"

"Absolutely," Lucas concurred with more gusto than he really felt.

He was about to add an afterthought when he noticed that Chet had turned his attention to a comely young waitress approaching them with decaf and regular coffeepots in hand.

"Say, honey," Chet grinned while slicking his hair back with one hand, "you're new here, aren't you?"

The very next morning Flora collared Lucas to ask him to talk some sense into Chet. *Why me?* Lucas wondered dizzily as he fumbled for the right words to blunt his wife's conviction, never an easy task. What he came up with was less than commanding: "Well honey, I have talked to Chet about Pierre lately. I have to admit that I think he might be right on this one. Maybe the boy needs to settle down a little bit before he..."

Flora cut off her husband with a cold stare and words that gave no quarter. "Never mind, Luke. I'll take care of it. I know how to handle Chet Townsend."

A distant explosion rattled the Jeep's windshield, making Lucas' heart race with fresh anticipation of the war zone they were approaching. He gave his driver a cheery thumbs-up sign, then sank rapidly into an acidic self-questioning.

Should he have seen it coming? Could he have? In the months following the awful discovery, Lucas would always torture himself with the utter banality of it all — how he found himself in the middle of the clichéd tale of the cuckolded husband, the poor dumb bastard who's so out of touch that he never sees it coming. In his own case, he heard it coming shortly before he saw it. Still, that was hardly sufficient preparation for the sight.

Even the circumstance of the discovery was hackneyed.

Lucas happened to leave classes early one day with a splitting headache, and drove home looking forward to a few hours' nap in the darkened bedroom. Then maybe a leisurely dinner out with his wife and daughter. He'd earned the right to skip out on an afternoon of teaching, that was for sure. When he entered the house, Wendy was nowhere to be found. The dining room was such a blizzard of unstuffed envelopes and uncurling rolls of postage that he turned away from the sight and began trudging slowly up the stairs.

He was about to call out for Flora when he heard her cry out instead. That single, obviously sexual cry told him everything. He paused, one hand tightening on the wooden stair rail, and waited a few chilling seconds for her next cry: "*Oh, God*" — and then the next, "Oh yes, honey, just like that!"

Like what? Lucas found himself wondering in a panic. Then he realized that he held the course of his life in his hands. If he quietly turned away and retreated down the stairs, there was a possibility of saving his marriage, his closest friendship, and a sense of normalcy in his life — at least for a little while. If he continued upstairs toward confrontation, he was likely risking it all. His deeply inbred caution told him to back down, go take a drive for an hour, come back home like nothing had happened. But an irrepressible rush of sick curiosity wanted to know the answer to *Like what?* So he stepped carefully up the stairs and halfway down the hall to the bedroom until he had a line of sight to the bed through the half-open door.

The worst part was that Flora saw him immediately, yet said or did nothing. She was lying on her stomach, her generous rump up-ended by two pillows under her pelvis, her head turned to the side facing the bedroom doorway. When she saw Lucas she just smiled icily, then squeezed her eyes shut, grimacing with the force of the man pushing into her, shoving into her from behind. He pushed and shoved several more times before he collapsed over her fleshy buttocks and back, moaning "Oh Jesus" in a deeply gratified tone. Then he rose up slightly, rolled over her right side, spied Lucas staring at him from the hallway and sputtered "*Oh, Jesus!*" before falling off the bed and out of the husband's line of sight.

For Lucas it was the most horrible scene imaginable, however clichéd and laughable it might have been to an uninvolved audience. Later Lucas would have to admit to himself that even in the uninhibited throes of sexual congress — and even as he had fallen awkwardly to the floor with his flagging penis glistening in the afternoon sunlight — the subtly muscular frame of nineteen-year-old Pierre Townsend displayed an undeniable, magnetic grace.

CHAPTER 17

IT WAS a little after eleven when Tom and Cal returned to Bernard's salon to find Wendy sitting outside the shop on a bench, distractedly patting a mass of damp, loose curls that fell about halfway down her neck in the back. She was unused to feeling air on her skin back there.

"Hey, cutie, look at you!" Tom crowed as the men came to stand in front of her, beaming and exchanging looks of self-congratulation.

Wendy looked up at her friends with one hand still on her head. "Bernard said it would *poof up* a little when it dries. He didn't have time to…"

"It looks great!" Cal enthused, holding out one hand to lift Wendy from the bench. "Now for the rest of this little expedition. Tom and I have scouted out the hottest shopping destinations in downtown Santa Rosa. After we finish with that we can grab lunch or go straight to the hospital, whichever you prefer." Wendy failed to reply, having become absorbed with digging in her purse to retrieve Cal's change from the two twenties he had pressed into Bernard's hands earlier. Cal resumed, "I mean, we really should get back to the hospital by early afternoon. I'll keep checking in by phone, but we don't know exactly when…"

"Oh, of course!" Wendy exclaimed as she found some crumpled bills and gave them to Cal. "I want to go. I'm not afraid now."

"Good," Cal said. "Let's move on."

For Wendy, the next two hours were far more than an exploration of an unknown commercial district. Under the watchful eyes and forceful direction of Cal and Tom, she felt that she was trailblazing a whole new territory inside herself as well — a territory of sensuous textures, colors, and shapes that she had never allowed herself to venture into. Of course she had been shopping before; until her mid-teens her mother had irregularly dragged her out for expeditions that netted a wild array of brightly colored and generally anachronistic fashions, as though Flora were attempting to costume her daughter for an upcoming production. Wendy would wear strange assemblages of the antique clothing once or twice to school, but she could not long endure the cruel stares and snickers of her peers.

By her second year in high school she had discovered the convenience and anonymity of black pants and her father's white shirts, and stubbornly refused to try anything else. Flora let her be after a while, apparently finding Pierre and Romero to be sublime shopping companions. Often at breakfast Wendy and Lucas would be sitting at the kitchen table wearing the same shirts fresh out of their wrappings, still shipped regularly as clockwork by Gramma Aggie. Lucas would wink at his daughter and say "That's my girl" while Flora shook her head in dismay. She did not seem to understand that the shirts were one of the few means Wendy had for feeling close to her father.

An amiable friction pervaded the whole shopping trip, beginning when Cal insisted that Wendy buy two pairs of shoes at a women's footwear boutique inside the Santa Rosa Plaza. Compared to the cloth sandals she was used to wearing, everything looked terribly expensive. Cal kept shaking his head firmly when Wendy drifted toward a small display of athletic walking shoes. He had found a pair of navy blue pumps with short, chunky heels that he liked for Wendy. But when she tried them on she wobbled, and not just because of the slight elevation of the heels. She felt too much like an oversized Cinderella who had no business trying on magic slippers.

But Cal was adamant. They compromised on the purchase of the pumps and one pair of sensible walkers that he allowed her to wear out of the shoe department — "at least until we find something to go with the good shoes," he directed. When the clerk slipped Wendy's old sandals into the walkers' box, Wendy grabbed for them but Cal intervened, pushing the box back to the clerk.

"Stick a fork in 'em," he said gruffly. "They're done."

At Macy's they found a sundress and a pantsuit, just as Cal had noted on his wish list. Wendy balked briefly at the idea of getting any kind of dress, confessing to her companions that she'd always assumed a dress would make her look even bigger than she was. Draped over a chair while watching the sundressed Wendy rotate uncertainly in front of a mirror, Tom had erupted in a Kid-like voice, "Big's okay. Little's okay. What's not okay?"— causing both Wendy and Cal to start toward him with concerned looks. But he had raised both his hands to stop them, protesting in a lower voice, "I'm okay! I'm okay!"

Wendy left the women's wear department clad in a dark blue knit pantsuit whose tunic and pants shared a subtle moon-and-stars pattern. It would have benefited from minor alterations, but Cal was insistent that Wendy immediately make the change from her old clothing — whose disposal Cal assured with a knowing nod to the salesgirl. On the way out of Macy's Wendy kept feeling the fine fabric on her sleeves with her fingers, stumbling occasionally from that distraction and the new pumps. Cal had insisted she switch shoes to coordinate with the outfit.

Heading toward the center part of town again to find a quick lunch, the trio happened upon a frilly shop window advertising *Unmentionables*, and Cal peered in through the glass to comment, "Looks like the hometown Victoria's Secret. Go for it, girl," he commanded, pushing Wendy toward the door.

"Oh no, Cal," Wendy protested, craning her neck to look up and down the street for some familiar signage. "I can always get underwear at Ross."

"Oh no you can't," he insisted. "Go in there and make us proud. In the meantime, we men will keep peace in the streets of Santa Rosa."

Wendy sighed and shrugged her shoulders, ceding the final skirmish to Cal along with all the others. After she had disappeared into the land of lingerie, Cal and Tom loitered aimlessly on the sidewalk with thumbs hooked in their belt loops like a couple of cowboys waiting for the saloon to open. After a while Tom broke from the manly posing to tug on Cal's sleeve like a son to his father, asking impishly, "So how come *foundations* are also *unmentionables*?" When she exited the shop a few minutes later with a new shopping bag in hand, Wendy found her shopping assistants in another slapping fight.

Shortly after one o'clock the three friends found themselves across the street again from Starbucks, this time at a corner deli which Cal quickly determined to have the pedigree of local ownership. By this time Wendy was spacing out, mumbling incoherently to herself with a secret smile. Cal seated her as if she were an elderly grandmother, glancing back at her frequently from the line where he and Tom went to order some light sandwiches. "She's going out on us again," he murmured to his partner. "Do you think she's all right?"

Tom's eyes did not stray from the menu board in front of him, yet he spoke as if he were reading an x-ray of Wendy's innards. "Oh, she's doing just fine. Making terrific progress today." Cal stared at Tom and shook his head, deciding for the thousandth time that he did not want to know about every source of information Tom was privy to.

At the table, Wendy was patting the soft cloth covering her arm and marveling at how nice it felt to her. "Nice," she mumbled for the tenth time, struck by the ever-deepening dimensions of a thoroughly ordinary word. Although she had faced the shopping trip with no little trepidation and then resisted Cal's direction at almost every step, she had been surprised by how pleasant the experience turned out to be — and how simple it was to find herself clothed in something *nice*.

In fact it was more than nice. Wendy felt wrapped in kindness, wreathed in respect, enfolded in a precious peacefulness. She was acutely aware of how rare and tender these feelings were — she wasn't even sure she had ever felt them before — and how easily she could smash them into nothingness with just the slightest surge of old-Wendy self-doubt and recrimination. But why would she treat herself that way, when kindness was as close as putting on a new suit of clothes?

"Got you a turkey and Swiss," Cal said solicitously as he took a seat across from Wendy, breaking into her reverie. "Hope that's okay."

Wendy turned her head robotically as Tom took the seat beside her, his eyes trained eagerly on his own sandwich. She grabbed his arm and blurted, "I'm not very nice!"

"Aw, Wendy," Cal responded across the way, more than a trace of exasperation in his voice.

"No, I mean I'm not very nice to *myself*!" Wendy explained angrily, her grip tightening on Tom's forearm until he winced. She didn't mean to be hurting him, but suddenly she needed an anchor against the landslide roaring through her heart. She was terrifically angry with herself for never seeing the simplicity of being nice, the ease of kindness, the naturalness of taking care. Of course she knew how to indulge herself, but indulgence always called for punishment afterward. Of course she knew how to think obsessively of herself and all her problems — but that entailed becoming so bored with Wendy Palmer that she could spend days in forgetfulness and distraction. Of course she knew how to hate herself; that's why she had to wallow in self-pity. In her perpetual battle between inner extremes, she had never seen the peace that lay in the simple middle, in the gentle laying-down of arms taken up against herself so long ago.

And that's when the most shattering of all the realizations Wendy had encountered in the last day came upon her: *there was no good reason for her inner battling*. Until that moment she thought she hated herself because she was ugly, fat, and isolated. With a chill so massive that she literally shook in her seat, Wendy realized that none of these causes justified her anger; in fact she hated herself for no reason at all. Her hatred was a rootless madness, a war against her own being governed only by the laws of chaos.

Wendy grabbed Tom's arm with her other hand and thrust her face into his with total abandon. "I'm a lunatic!" she seethed. "I'm totally insane!"

Smiling at her eye to eye, Tom didn't miss a beat. "Who isn't?"

he replied calmly. "Want some?" he added, raising his ham sandwich to Wendy's face like a lion trainer rewarding his beast.

But it was not Wendy's moment to be pacified. Tom's simple revelation laid her open like a knife; she felt the fresh pain of a grief deeper than she had ever known. Tom was right. The madness in her was not hers alone, but the madness of just about everybody. Although she had seen a lot of suffering on the TV news and in the faces of people on the street — in the faces of her own father and mother, for that matter — she had never related this suffering to her own, which had always been more special somehow, utterly unique and irresolvable. As the cold stone boundaries between her pain and the world's pain began to crumble, Wendy felt the unmovable mountain of herself beginning to collapse and disintegrate, tumbling like boulders into a mighty river of being that joined her with everyone.

She grabbed Tom all the way around and laid her head against his chest, bawling out loud as she had never bawled before, her chest heaving and her feet madly stamping the floor. She was drawing the shocked and silent attention of everyone in the deli. As she moaned and wailed, her weeping so intense that she was soon gasping loudly for breath, Tom calmly encircled Wendy's shoulders with one arm and patted her head with his other hand, smiling beatifically at Cal as if all were going according to plan.

Transfixed by the sight of Wendy losing her grip in a big way, Cal sat still without touching his food for several minutes while her sobbing rose and fell, finally subsiding to a muffled huffing against Tom's chest. When an electronic *threep* sounded in Cal's pocket, he reached automatically for his cell phone. Locking eyes with Tom, he listened intently while saying only "Yes" three times softly during a half-minute. Cal then folded the phone and slipped it back into his pocket. He stood and reached over to touch Wendy's shoulder.

"Wendy," he said with a grave kindness, "that was the hospital. We'd better get over there now."

Chapter 18

RECOLLECTING the bitterly distasteful vision of Flora and Pierre copulating sent Lucas into a blind fit of rage. He snarled at his obedient young driver — "Son, can't you make this crate go any faster?" — then shifted in his seat to place his wingtip over the soldier's boot, pressing the accelerator of the Jeep to the metal flooring.

"Watch out, sir!" the driver shrieked, jerking the wheel to the left just in time to avoid driving under the high carriage of the munitions truck in front of them. The army had been plodding through the streets of Sacramento for about ten minutes. When the Jeep pulled out of line it careened over a sidewalk and right into a streetlamp, launching both Lucas and his young attendant into the air over the collapsing windshield. Lucas landed and rolled in the soft grass of a mowed front lawn. The driver's body hit the metal pole of the streetlamp with a sickening crunch and then tumbled to the concrete walk.

For Lucas everything went black for a timeless moment, his only sensation being a faintly remembered sinking through inky-dark liquid. Then his awareness returned with an electric shock, and he sprang to his feet to fix his coordinates. Fifteen feet away the young driver lay in a contorted, mortally silent heap. "Sorry, son," Lucas mumbled coldly, "this is war."

He began running toward the reverberating shocks and billowing smoke of massive explosions that appeared to be taking place no more than a half-mile to the west. Soon Lucas had gained the territory of the neighborhood where he had spent most of his childhood and his adult life as well. All around him, it was clear that the 3RD Army had done as much damage simply by arriving as they could have achieved with a full-scale assault. Trees, fire hydrants, and street signs had been mowed down by tanks and trucks; bucolic gardens and sundecks had been commandeered by the set-up of artillery positions; the dazed neighbors had been hustled out of their homes to make way for command posts, radio operation centers, mobile hospitals, and impromptu mess halls.

The whole area had been conquered by a roaming culture of violence, and Lucas felt energized by the bizarre transformation of the so-familiar territory. Before this moment, none of his neighbors would have ever guessed that there could be trouble brewing inside the home of the placid professor, his actressy wife, and their chunky daughter. *They sure as hell know there's big trouble now*, Lucas thought with satisfaction.

As the professor raced breathlessly around the corner to his own block, he spied a high wall of fortifications just beyond a shallow trench dug into the jack-hammered pavement of the street fronting his own yard. As he dove for cover into a spot beside the crouching General Patton, he got a glance of his house — or at least the hellish tornado of smoke and flame that was enveloping it. The house was surrounded and taking hits from all sides, making it difficult to hear Patton's orders to his officers through the vicious din. When he noticed Lucas beside him, the General roughly clapped a helmet onto his skull and pulled him close.

"You made it, sonny!" he bellowed. "I knew you'd be here when push came to shove. The enemy held us off for a while, but we've got her cornered now. She's got nowhere to run!" He paused long enough to grab a radio and shout some coordinates into it. Moments later a fresh wave of mortar fire screamed overhead and poured into the half-acre that comprised the Palmer estate. Lucas briefly wondered how anything could be left of Flora and the house by this point. There had never even been a gun in the house and he'd put off buying a burglar alarm system for years. There was something ludicrous about this scene, but he couldn't quite put his finger on it.

At any rate, this was no time for analysis. Fearing that he might not get his shots in before the fight was over, Lucas shouted, "What can I do, sir? Where do you need me?"

Patton wheeled about and lifted something off the ground behind him, then turned again and slammed a picnic basket into Lucas' gut. It was the same basket in which Flora had gathered the diamonds of his consciousness. Besides the few that Patton had used earlier for target practice, they were apparently all there. "Grab that grenade launcher over there, sonny!" Patton directed. "Drop a few of these babies down her gullet. That will damn sure get her attention, if nothing else does."

Lucas dipped one hand into the glassy gems and tumbled a few from his palm, still not quite understanding their connection to his own mind. Flora had seemed quite adamant about protecting them. He had the vague intimation that they provided a crucial link to — *what*? He closed his eyes and briefly saw the diamonds strung together on a glossy thread, stretching infinitely into a watery darkness. When he tried to see farther, he was surprised to hear Flora's voice in his head, calmly instructing, "Save them. Save them for a lifeline."

That did it. Lucas opened his eyes to see Patton staring at him, looking as red-eyed and dangerous as a rabid wolf, growling "Well, son? Are you in this man's war or not?"

"Yes, sir!" Lucas shouted, commencing to load the diamonds into the launcher and fire them — *thrump, thrump, thrump* — as fast as he could manage. If Flora thought the diamonds were something precious, then he wanted to show her they meant nothing to him. If one of the heavy stones happened to thunk her soundly on the head, so much the better. For now he wanted to send Flora a message that he had failed to send her years before.

IT WAS not that he never planned to show her exactly how he felt about her infidelity. In fact a plan of action was already forming the moment he had begun backing away from the ugly scene in their bedroom, hearing no pleas from his wife, only those of her young lover at his back: "Uh, Dr. Palmer, sir? Wait, sir! It's not like you think..."

Spare me the clichés, Lucas had thought bitterly, deliberately reversing the path he had taken into the house only minutes earlier. He picked up his jacket from the kitchen table and fingered his briefcase momentarily before deciding to leave it. Waiting one last second for a word from Flora, he then took the keys to his Mercedes from the hook in the entry hallway and left the house. He closed the door behind him with extra caution, as if he were sneaking out in the middle of the night.

Lucas drove straight to his favorite branch of the Men's Wearhouse, asking a salesman there to fit him with the finest suit in the place, sparing no expense as long as he could be taken care of on the spot without alterations. That proved to be no problem. Within forty minutes Lucas was zooming over the Bay Bridge toward San Francisco feeling like a new man on the outside, and a potent charge of explosive on the inside.

"I *guarantee* it," Lucas kept mumbling to himself, imitating the unforgettable twang of the Men's Wearhouse founder he had heard so many times on radio commercials as he made his daily commute to the University. "I guarantee it." *At least somebody around here is reliable,* Lucas thought bitterly.

In the City he parked at the Stockton-Sutter garage and ambled into the bright, breezy, tourist-clogged ambience of Union Square on an autumn afternoon. He made his first attempt to find a room at the Sir Francis Drake, where he and Flora had consummated their love affair so many years before. That hotel was booked. One block away he found an expensive, absurdly large suite at the St. Francis, then idled around the gift shop buying a toothbrush, throwaway razor, and everything else he would need for an impromptu weekend away from home. He fingered a plastic vial of aspirins before realizing, with a note of victory, that the splitting headache which had driven him from work had disappeared.

By the time he deposited his small treasure of sundries in the room it was nearly seven p.m. He made his way to the hotel's finest restaurant to treat himself to a gourmet dinner. He prided himself on how collected he was in the aftermath of a discovery that surely would have shattered a man of less composure. Nonetheless he decided to move his wine glass closer to the edge of the table, so that less of the fine vintage spilled each time he shakily lifted the fluted crystal to his lips.

Afterward he retired to the St. Francis tea room, situated one short flight of stairs up from the grand lobby. He ordered a fine sherry and contemplated the execution of the remainder of his instinctive plan.

Not being the worldliest of men, he was unclear on the most efficient means of procuring the services of a high-class call girl. He wished that he could call Chet Townsend for a few pointers, but all things considered, such a call would entail too much explanation. And perhaps he shouldn't disabuse his old friend of the notion that Lucas Palmer was entirely straight and narrow.

Lucas did know that there were plenty of disreputable girls for hire just a few blocks away, but he also knew his limitations. He had no desire to be found dead and dishonored in a Tenderloin alley the next morning. "My way or the highway," he whispered nonsensically, taking a sip of the sherry in the tearoom's evening shadows, grinning like a madman.

Finally he hit upon a method that guaranteed his safety and had a certain poetic justice to it as well. He remembered that after the disastrous flop of one of Flora's shows, she had started talking about "creating a new reality" for her next debut. Apparently she believed that she could draw the size and quality of audience she desired simply by creating an internal vision of what she wanted to see beyond the footlights. *Never mind putting on a better show,* Lucas had thought condescendingly, but he had only smiled indulgently at his wife at the time.

But now, something that Flora had said about "drawing the goal of your intention toward you" made perfect sense to Lucas in his state of mild inebriation. At any rate it was worth a try. He would just sit there in the tearoom lounge and meditate on the vision of a seductive, sophisticated professional lady of the night who would seek him out without knowing why. Even if she usually plied her trade in a cheaper hotel, she would magically be drawn to the St. Francis by Lucas' intention. He would show Flora a thing or two about creating reality.

Lucas must have dozed off during his righteous reverie, for the next thing he was aware of was a woman's voice calling to him from the plush sofa situated next to his chair. She sounded insistent, even a little exasperated. "Suh, I *said*, ah you with the sales convention?" The Southern accent was similar enough to Flora's that Lucas bolted awake with a flush to his cheeks, before seeing that the lady sitting in the loveseat aside his chair bore no resemblance whatsoever to his wife. She was blonde and bony, with sharp cheekbones, watery blue eyes and thin, crimson-red lips that were leaving a noticeable print on the gin glass she held unsteadily in one hand.

"Excuse me?" Lucas responded, straightening his posture and blinking his eyes, noticing that the thin woman didn't look too bad for her age — probably about the same as his — and was wearing a plastic nametag with a corporate logo identifying her as Mrs. Russell Sullivan, SPOUSE. "I'm sorry, I must have dozed off for a second. I've had a little more to drink than I'm accustomed to."

"Me too," she smiled woozily, then knocked back the remaining liquid in her glass and raised her hand like a schoolchild, waving her fingers at a distant waiter.

"Anyhow, Mrs. Sullivan," Lucas said with a polite nod toward her nametag, "no, I'm not with a sales convention. I'm a professor from the University of California at..."

"Oh my!" Mrs. Sullivan exclaimed. "Finally, someone intelligent ah can talk to. What are you in town for, Professuh...?"

"Martin," Lucas replied, thinking fast. "Royal Martin, professor emeritus in the geographic sciences at, uh, UCLA. I've just come into town for a weekend consultation with some colleagues here for a major study of meta-geography. You see, in my field we've never put together the big picture that..."

"Oh my, oh my," Mrs. Sullivan interrupted with a birdlike cooing. "That certainly sounds so important." A slight, middle-aged Korean waiter appeared and she spoke slowly and loudly to him as if he were a child: "I, will, have, anothuh, *gin*, please?"

"Yes, ma'am," he replied without a trace of an accent. "And you, sir?"

Lucas peered at his nearly-empty sherry glass and said, "I'll have what the lady is having. And please, place it on my tab. Suite 443."

"Oh my," the blonde purred again. "That's very sweet, Professuh Roy. And do call me Ellen," she added, setting down her glass to clumsily finger her nametag, almost ripping her silk blouse in the process. Lucas leaned forward to assist. She finally pulled the pin loose on her own and slammed the tag name-down on the table in front of her.

"So Ellen," Lucas ventured, "you're here with your husband at a sales convention?"

"Well Roy," she replied shakily, "now the funny thing about that is that he's *spozed* to be heah, but ah swear ah haven't seen him all the livelong day. Ain't that the damndest thing? Come all the way from Texas to spend some time with your husband and he just *disappears!*" She tittered in a high, silly tone, and then her face abruptly turned grave.

"Oh, I see," Lucas replied uncertainly. "Was he called away for...?"

Ellen stared straight ahead and began speaking as if she were by herself. "Ah *told* him he wasn't goin' away with that whore secretary one more time if ah had anything to do with it. Ah *told* him ah would just come along on his next business trip, and see the sights in San Francisco right along with him. So what does he do? He puts up that tart somewheah else and just takes off with her. Leaves me sittin' around this hotel all damn day and night like a dingbat." She turned her head and seemed to notice Lucas again. "That's such a nice suit, Professuh Roy. Ah wish my husband had yoah good taste."

Lucas slowly closed his eyes and heaved a big sigh before answering. "Uh, yes, Ellen. Thank you very much. I just bought this suit this afternoon, for the conference."

"Well, it's very nice," she repeated, then added in a faltering voice, "Professuh?"

"Yes?"

"My husband ain't comin' back heah tonight. Ah know it."

"Well, perhaps you should wait and see."

"Oh no, that bastard won't be back. He just had to do it this way, don't you see? Always makes it hurt the worst possible way, that sonuvabitch. Ah think he's more cruel than his mama, and now that's *sayin'* sumthin'. . ."

Lucas shifted uncomfortably in his seat, looking left and right for an escape hatch. The woman apparently noticed his movements and reached for her purse, then rose to her feet unsteadily. "Mrs. Sullivan?" Lucas asked quizzically.

She curled an index finger at Lucas and he rose in response. She placed both hands on his shoulders and pulled shockingly close to him, whispering in his ear, "Why don't we go to mah room, Professuh Roy? I just *luv* that suit."

Lucas laughed in spite of himself and said gently, "Okay, Mrs. Sullivan, let's go." He put one arm around her waist and escorted her down the stairway toward the lobby elevators.

"Oh, yoah s'sweet," she slurred. "You would never leave me alone all the livelong day, now would you?"

"No, Mrs. Sullivan," he assured her. "That's a terrible thing to do. Your husband should be ashamed. Let's have a look at your room key, okay?"

Giggling, Ellen Sullivan fished around in her purse as the pair entered an elevator. Lucas held open the door until she produced the key and he could read the number. When they got to the sixth floor, he ushered the stumbling woman to her room, unlocked the door, and called out "Mr. Sullivan, sir?" before flicking on the lights and leading Ellen to the bed.

"Heah we ahh," Ellen said in a sexy swoon, dropping her thin frame on the corner of the bed and beginning to unbutton her blouse. Lucas knelt to slip off her shoes and when that was done he moved to the head of the bed, turning down the cover and fluffing up one pillow. Ellen stood unsteadily and slipped off her skirt so that she was wearing only her underwear. Lucas grimaced at the sight of her prominent ribcage and concave stomach.

"That's fine, now," he said gently, and helped Ellen slip under the covers. She mumbled something unintelligible about "Russell" and seemed to be fading into sleep immediately before her blue eyes opened wide and she said in a frightened voice, "Are you coming back? Will you be heah for dinnuh?"

Lucas smiled sadly and replied, "Sleep it off, Mrs. Sullivan. Russell will be back soon, I'm sure."

"Thass nice," she mumbled, and was soon fast asleep. Lucas turned out the light, left the key on top of a dresser and stepped quietly out the door, pausing briefly afterward to stare blankly at the number. "Scarecrow," he whispered disdainfully before trudging heavily down the hallway to the elevator.

The next morning Lucas had somehow expected to awaken feeling normal. He was shocked to find himself in a heavy depression instead. He checked out of the hotel in a blur, walked to his car and drove out of the garage to wander aimlessly up and down the streets of San Francisco, noticing little that he could make out under the morning fog. He drove through Golden Gate Park to the wide avenue before the ocean, and sat there staring at the vague gray skyline for half an hour. He was trying to summon the resolve to return to Sacramento and figure out the rest of his life, but he had no plan of action.

In a fugue of melancholy Lucas started the car again and drove slowly into the lower Sunset, happening onto a small commercial district where he pulled the car over when he spotted a sign for a pawn shop. On a hunch, he entered the store just as its proprietor, a frizzy-haired fellow with thick glasses and a cigar, appeared to be going into a back office. Lucas hailed him and asked if he had any pistols for sale. The shop owner looked longingly toward the back and then asked Lucas if he knew what he was looking for in particular.

"No," Lucas replied uncertainly, "just some kind of small handgun. For self-protection, you know."

The proprietor eyed the man in the sharp suit skeptically before bending down behind a counter, unlocking something and then producing a long tray with six handguns arrayed across it, all attached by small chains to the back of the counter. "Here, take a look at these," he said hurriedly. "I gotta go to the can. I'll be right back."

Lucas picked up a cheap gun with imitation ivory plates on its handgrip and hefted it. He had never picked up a gun before in his life. He raised it as far as the chain would allow, vaguely aiming at the glass case of cameras and electronic goods across from him. Then the tears began to come. He stared at the gun in a blur and slowly raised it toward his face, inserting the barrel into his mouth and closing his lips around it. The gun tasted rank and metallic on his tongue as water flowed profusely from the professor's eyes.

There was a toilet flush in the back and the proprietor shortly re-emerged, saw Lucas holding the gun in this mouth and exclaimed, "What the hell are you doing, you sick fuck? Like I need a nutcase in here along with the rest of my problems." He scurried over to Lucas and brusquely pulled the gun away from him, slamming it back on the tray and lowering the tray back where it had come from. "You wanna kill yourself, go try the Golden Gate Bridge. It's right over that way!" He pointed out the door, then waved Lucas off.

Lucas left the shop without a word and drove the Mercedes over to the tourists' parking lot for the City end of the Golden Gate. He shouldered his way through a gaggle of Japanese tourists on the cold walk up to the bridge. The biting wind off the ocean cut right through the fabric of his suit. He walked only a short way before pausing to lean against the cold railing of the bridge, trying to peer through the grating to the dark green waters below. Lucas knew he would never jump, just as he would never have bought that handgun. For the professor knew himself to be incapable of dramatic actions. He was mild to the core; ultimately he would cave in and accept whatever unfairness life decided to hand to him.

On the long drive back to Sacramento on that gray Saturday, that was exactly what Lucas Palmer decided to do. He doubted that Flora would continue sleeping with Pierre Townsend — he wondered hopefully, in fact, if perhaps he had stumbled into their first and only sexual encounter, some kind of freakish, momentary intimacy between a young homosexual and the older woman he probably loved more than his own mother.

Perhaps Pierre was being truthful when he had wailed, "It's not what you think!"

That must be it, Lucas decided, and if so, that was forgivable. Things would sort themselves out somehow. He and Flora would start talking again, clear the air between them, and get on with life. It would have to be that way, Lucas decided, simply because he could not imagine life without Flora — and he could not imagine how his daughter would manage without the two of them. She barely had a life as it was.

That observation was solidly confirmed when Lucas arrived home in the mid-afternoon, his headache of twenty-fours before back in full force. When he entered the house he could hear the television blaring. Two open cereal packages sat on the kitchen table along with a carton of milk. Several envelopes and copies of recipes were strewn on the floor between the dining room and the TV room, where Wendy had apparently transplanted the mail-order mess in order not to make any progress with it there either. Shaking his head at the chaos and wondering if Flora was about, Lucas heard the toilet flush upstairs and then Wendy's heavy steps descending the stairs. When she turned from the hallway into the kitchen and saw her father, Wendy blurted, "Where have you guys been? Mom left early this morning without saying a word, and you didn't even come home last night, Daddy!"

Lucas eyed his daughter testily. "Stop whining, Wendy, and clean up this mess. I swear to God, you're a twenty-one-year-old woman now and you still act like a child."

Wendy began to tear up, biting her lower lip. "Daddy," she wailed, "I'm only twenty!"

THRUMP. Lucas launched the last of the big sparkling diamonds into the air, and watched it sail in a high arc into the chaos of smoke and fire that enveloped his house. "Cease fire!" Patton shouted into his radio, and Lucas heard the order repeated several times around him until the mortar fire, the rifle fire, and the fire of the tanks encircling the besieged residence all fell silent. "Let's see what's left of her fortifications now," Patton remarked smugly, and stood to train his binoculars on the scene before them.

Lucas felt empty — just as he had felt when standing in the house confronting Wendy on that Saturday afternoon years before, and just as he would for many weeks to follow that. Late that evening Flora drove in; she had the Chevy station wagon they had bought from Townsend's used lot not long after the Mercedes. She came into the house silently with a load of groceries. Lucas was in his study upstairs reclining in his big chair with the lights off, and pretended to be asleep. When there was a soft knock on the door, he first ignored it. When Flora knocked twice, he said "Yes? Is that you, Flora?"

She pushed open his door halfway and said without entering, "We're going to have to talk, Lucas. I'm terribly sorry about yesterday, but I don't think you understand what you saw. I don't think you've tried to understand anything about me for a long time."

Lucas was silent for a few moments, then spoke in a deliberately weakened voice. "We'll have to talk later, Flo. I don't feel very well right now. I've had a terrible headache since *before* I came home yesterday." Lucas was not facing his wife as he spoke. He made no attempt to turn in his chair.

Now there was a long silence on Flora's part. "I'm sorry, dear," she said neutrally. "I hope you feel better soon." Then the door closed softly, and Lucas sighed heavily, feeling safe yet strangely ashamed.

Waiting for the smoke to clear from the bombardment of Flora, Lucas glanced over at the General and recalled how he'd been saved from making any decisions by Chet Townsend, a man of action. Chet had called on Monday night and in a low, urgent tone asked Lucas to a Tuesday morning breakfast, not the day of their regular habit. Sitting across from him in the booth that day, Lucas noticed that Chet was nervous as a cat, chattering stupidly about the weather before their food arrived and then, immediately after it was served to them, eyeing Lucas uncertainly with his jaw working back and forth. Finally he blurted, "Goddammit, Luke, we've gotta talk about Pierre and, uh, you know..."

"I know," Lucas replied evenly. "How do you know?"

Chet looked relieved, and started explaining immediately. "Boy came home Saturday looking like a walking heart attack. Said he thought you were comin' after him. I asked him why and he beat around the bush for about five minutes before he admitted the whole thing. And then he told me that you walked in on it. I can't tell you how sorry I am about this, Luke. This is a terrible, terrible thing. No man should have to put up with this."

"You didn't do anything, Chet," Lucas said mildly.

"No, but I feel like I did," he replied. Lucas raised one eyebrow. "I mean, he's my boy, he's my responsibility, and he should know better than — well, I know I'm not the best role model in the world. Anyway, I've taken care of everything."

"You have?" Lucas asked, mystified.

"Yeah. The funny thing is, I guess Pierre wins in the end. He's getting what he wanted after all."

"He is?"

"Yeah, now he can go be a goddamn famous dancer," Chet grumped. "Shipped him off to New York yesterday. So he's out of both our hair."

Chet's jaw was working furiously again. Lucas sensed that there was more to the story. "Chet?" he asked solicitously.

"Never laid a hand on my own flesh and blood before," Chet confessed, his eyes flickering nervously as he looked to Lucas for his reaction.

"You *hit* Pierre?" Lucas asked, genuinely shocked.

"Aw, it was nothing. Boy may be a great dancer but he can't take a punch." Chet socked the air with his fist. "One clean hit and he's down. So he'll go to his first audition with a shiner. Big fuckin' deal."

Lucas sat back in his seat, amazed at what he was feeling. "Thanks, Chet," he said truthfully.

"Nothin' to it," Chet responded coolly. "At least there's a silver lining to this whole mess," he added with a glint in his eye.

"Oh yeah, what's that?"

"I mean, at least I know my son's not a *complete* faggot!" Chet grinned wickedly and looked to Lucas once more for a sign of approval, getting only a dropped mouth at first. "Ha, ha, HA!" Chet boomed. Lucas joined in laughing in spite of himself, and soon they were both roaring, drawing all the eyes and ears of the patrons in the coffee shop.

LUCAS was still laughing when Patton grabbed him by the shoulder and barked, "What are *you* laughin' about, sonny?" He shoved Lucas around to face the house that had been under withering bombardment by the 3RD Army. Now that the smoke had mostly cleared, Lucas could see that while everything around his home had been blasted to bits, the structure itself was untouched, looking as fresh as the day it had been repainted in 1992, shortly before Flora had fallen ill. All the bullets, shells, and grenades — even the diamonds Lucas had launched into the fray — had done nothing, disappearing without a trace. Now Lucas felt sick about the diamonds, as if he had squandered his life's savings at an amusement park. When he faced Patton again, his laughter had yielded to a grim confusion.

"Doesn't look so funny now, eh?" Patton sneered.

Lucas looked back and forth from the house to the General, his sense of wrongness about the whole scene ramping up considerably. "But how…?" he wondered aloud.

"Goddamn aura," Patton said mysteriously. "She must have been holding the whole house in a white-light visualization." Patton laid his hand atop Lucas' helmet and pushed him roughly to the ground, behind the safety of their fortifications. "Hunker down, sonny, 'cause I'm afraid we're in for it now. She's gonna hit us with all she's got."

Chapter 19

WENDY'S cathartic sobbing continued to subside on the short trip to Santa Rosa Memorial, located about half a mile from where Tom, Wendy, and Cal had not been having their lunch. She was wiping her eyes and taking deep breaths by the time Cal turned the VW into the parking lot. He had explained that a nurse phoned to tell him Lucas was in trouble, and Dr. Chambers was coming in to monitor the situation.

Inside the lobby Cal seated Tom and Wendy, and told them to wait for him. He was not sure Wendy was prepared to be taken to the ICU. He started off down the hall, gazing worriedly at the floor. After about twenty feet he collided with a breathless Dr. Chambers striding in the opposite direction, his white jacket unbuttoned to reveal a Howard University sweatshirt.

"Oh, excuse me, Doctor," Cal apologized. "I was just on my way to look for you."

"And I for you," Chambers responded gravely. "Is Mr. Palmer's daughter here?"

"Yes," Cal responded, pointing down the hallway toward Tom and Wendy. The doctor peered intently in their direction, blinking his eyes at the young woman in a dark pantsuit, nice shoes, and a new hairdo.

"Is that Miss Palmer?" Dr. Chambers asked in disbelief.

"Oh, yeah," Cal replied with a proud smile. "She wasn't really looking like herself yesterday. You know, from the shock and all."

"Of course," the physician affirmed, still staring. Finally he broke his gaze and returned his attention to Cal. "Listen, I'm afraid we almost lost her father. His heart stopped and he had to be revived. I just got in here to have a look myself, and it doesn't look good. All his vitals are fluctuating, we're having a hard time stabilizing him. He's got a real battle going on, but I doubt he's going to win it. You should probably stick around until... well, until further notice."

"Can we go see him?" Cal inquired.

Chambers scratched his head before replying. "I suppose it would be all right for a minute or two. There's a nurse on duty right beside him. But we'll have to clear you out if there's an emergency. I'll leave it up to you at this point."

Cal gestured toward Tom and Wendy and led the doctor over to where they sat. Before Cal could speak the doctor extended a hand toward Wendy and said, "How nice to see you again, Miss Palmer, although I'm truly sorry about these circumstances. You're looking fine today, I must say."

Wendy blushed and stood as she held Dr. Chambers' hand, sneaking a sidewise, nervous smile at Tom. She returned her attention to the physician as she broke their handclasp and asked quietly, "How is my dad?"

Chambers took a long moment to stare at Wendy's hair before replying grimly. "Not good, I'm afraid. I was just telling your friend that he had a serious crisis about an hour ago. We had to restart his heart. He's under watch now, but to tell the whole truth, I'm not optimistic." Chambers paused again, then tentatively reached out one bearish hand to clasp Wendy on the shoulder. "You can wait out here if you like. I'll be here as long as I'm needed, and I can let you know if . . ."

"No," Wendy said decisively, turning aside to pick up her purse, doubling its strap in her palm to hide the tooth marks. "I should be there now."

HUNKERED down behind the battlements arrayed before his own house, Lucas looked wonderingly at General Patton and said, "What do you mean, she'll hit us with all she's got? Flora doesn't even have a gun."

Patton straightened up halfway from his stoop to peer cautiously over the fortifications, then returned to nose-to-nose intimacy with Lucas. "Yeah, but she's got a sound system to beat the band, sonny. She had us going for a while with those zingers of hers, before I opened fire and drowned her out."

"Zingers, sir?" Lucas questioned.

"Yeah, sonny, zingers — you know. Affirmations, proverbs, Zen koans, smart-ass sayings, all that crap. I've never seen anyone use positive thinking with such deadly accuracy."

Lucas' head was spinning. "Affirmations, sir? Flora held off the Third Army with *affirmations*? This doesn't make any sense!" By now Lucas was almost shouting his protest.

"Shhh, sonny," Patton chided him. "You'll give away our position. Now stay down and shut up. And you might want to cover your ears." Patton stuck his index fingers into his own ear canals, and squeezed his eyes shut in a cartoonish grimace.

"Oh, for the love of God," Lucas muttered, ready to stand up and be done with it. But he snapped to when he heard the audible click of a public address system, a few seconds of scratchy static, and then his wife's voice.

"Yoo-hoo, *Mr. General*, sir!" Flora's call floated airily over occupied Sacramento. "Don't you know that we could all see peace instead of this?"

Lucas glanced at the General, who had replaced his index fingers with the palms of his hands and seemed ready to push his two ears together, brains be damned. "Shut up, shut up, *shut up*," he was mumbling madly.

"We could all walk together in gratitude," Flora continued in a brassy yet prayerful tone. "Every day in every way, we're all getting better and better. One day at a time — and easy does it! If the only tool you have is a hammer, everything looks like a nail..."

"Shut up, bitch!" Patton screamed, flinging off his helmet and going for one of his pearl-handled revolvers. "I'll show you a goddamned nail!" But the General was fumbling, seemingly incapable of undoing the leather safety clasp over his gun. When Lucas leaned down to look closer, he could see that Patton's eyes were streaming with tears, and his whole body was shaking.

"Forgiveness offers everything you could possibly want," Flora declaimed, and the General fell in a heap on the ground, sobbing uncontrollably. Lucas squatted over him and shook his shoulder.

"All right, sir," Lucas said firmly, "enough of this nonsense. I'm going in there myself. I'm finally beginning to understand what's going on around here."

Patton clutched greedily at Lucas' shirt and regarded him with a wild, frightened glare. "Don't do it, son. Don't sacrifice yourself. No poor dumb bastard ever won a war by dying for his country. You win the war by making the *other* poor dumb bastard die for..."

Lucas put a finger to Patton's mouth and said firmly, "With all due respect, General Patton — sir — stick a sock in it." Then Lucas stood, clambered over the battlements, and called out, "Flora!"

"Luke, is that you?" she replied, her voice amplified but wavery. "Luke honey, I need you."

Luke honey, I need you. The words slowed Lucas in his tracks as he suddenly recalled the scenario in which he had heard that exact phrase so many times: the final act of Flora's life. It had begun a few years after the horrendous episode with Pierre — a few years spent in a dull, going-through-the-motions simulacrum of life. Flora and Lucas never talked about the sex episode because Lucas wanted it forgotten and Flora seemed vanquished in its aftermath. In Pierre's absence she soon closed her theater company and stuck grimly to her schoolteaching while Lucas continued his unremarkable career at the University. Wendy got out of the mail-order business, and occasionally got herself out of the house to look for work. But in general the whole family settled into a kind of mid-life torpor resting unhealthily on a foundation of untold secrets. Just as she would never be told her real age, Wendy would never be told of her mother's indiscretion with Pierre Townsend.

But at least some of the Palmer silences were broken after the onset of Flora's cancer. One morning when Lucas was brushing his teeth he heard Flora call from the bedroom, "Luke honey, I need you!" There was an odd, panicky twinge to her voice, enough to make him forget about rinsing and attend to her call immediately. When he entered the bedroom he saw Flora facing him dressed only in her panties, her full, exposed breasts looking as alluring to him as ever. Lucas briefly wondered if she was trying to be sexy, trying to revive the intimate physical life between them that was now virtually extinguished. But Flora had one hand up under her left breast and a look on her face betraying equal parts of fear and puzzlement.

"Luke honey," she repeated, "I think I have a lump?"

The cataclysm fell upon Lucas and Flora Palmer with the unannounced finality of a roof caving in. Flora never had a chance, as revealed by the diagnosis of an aggressive, rapidly metastasizing cancer that was already making inroads into her lymph glands by the time she caught the lump. From the first meeting with an oncologist held a week later, Flora was given a grim prognosis of six months. She would hold on three months longer than that.

Those were the three months she elected to spend at home without further medical intervention, turning the Palmer residence into a hospice that hosted a regular stream of whispery visitors: volunteer caretakers, therapists and healers, weepy high school students, Chet Townsend and his new wife Stephanie, and, near the end, Pierre. By virtue of the frequent presence of guests in the house — guests who could only spend a limited amount of time with the person they came to see — Wendy almost developed a social life during her mother's decline.

And Lucas developed an openness with his wife that had eluded them for all the years of his marriage. Even so, the change owed mostly to Flora's initiative. With the natural authority bestowed upon her by the nearness of death, she began calling Lucas into her room with regularity and talking freely of the past, discharging herself of a lifetime of unfinished business while Lucas listened attentively. He never said much, but smiled warmly and faithfully patted his wife's pale hand or wiped feverish beads of sweat from her brow as she remembered and reflected.

Pierre showed up just a few weeks from the end, fresh off a successful performance as the lead dancer in an off-Broadway production that was garnering some significant reviews. Flora was obviously happy to see him. But Pierre was a nervous wreck, flitting in and out of the house over the first few days like a butterfly dodging a net. Lucas finally caught up with him in the foyer and told him firmly that he should feel welcome in the house, that the past was over — as Flora was so fond of saying — and that all was forgiven.

Lucas didn't quite know if he meant it all even as he said it. Yet he somehow knew it was the right thing to do, as right as putting Ellen Sullivan safely to bed on the worst night of his life. Pierre looked visibly relieved and began staying at the house for hours at a time, talking up Wendy and sharing tales of the New York performer's life with the whole family when they would gather for lap-held dinners in Flora's room each evening. Lucas could well imagine that Pierre did not have quite as friendly or informed an audience at home.

"Luke honey, I need you," Flora called Lucas one morning about a week after Pierre's arrival, her voice floating airily downstairs from the bedroom. Lucas excused himself from an awkward meeting with a well-meaning local minister and hurried up the stairs. As was often the case, the husband found his ailing wife propped up in bed with her well-thumbed, blue-bound copy of *A Course in Miracles* open on her lap.

"Don't make fun," she pleaded, "this is really helping me today."

"When have I ever made fun of you?" Lucas replied with chagrin, sitting on the side of the bed.

"I'm sorry," Flora conceded, "that's right. You've never been one to have a cruel tongue. But sometimes you say everything on your mind by not saying anything, dear. That's just your way."

"Hmm," Lucas sighed.

"Anyway, dear, I just wanted to thank you for being so nice to Pierre. It does my heart good to see him on his way, and I guess you would have every right to show him the door. But I don't think you ever understood what was going on."

"Hush, Flo," Lucas admonished, "we don't have to go over ancient history now."

Flora sat up straighter in bed, wincing from the bandages wrapped around her midsection, and shook a finger at Lucas like a schoolmarm. "Oh yes we do, Lucas Palmer. I'm not going to pass on and leave something like this undone. I wasn't having a big affair with Pierre, Luke. For God's sake he was only nineteen, and more than a little confused about his sexuality."

Lucas wanted to say *he sure didn't look confused to me*, but held his tongue. Flora tilted her head at something she saw on her husband's face, but let it pass. "We just slept together a few times," she continued in a near-whisper. "It would happen when he needed some reassurance — he didn't get very much at home, you know, especially after Monique left — and when I got a little too lonely, I guess."

"Flo," Lucas protested, "you've always had people around you most of the time."

Flora rolled her eyes. "I meant when I got lonely for you, Luke. Do you remember the time you were running for that University Senate post — you know, that political thing?"

"Yes," Lucas replied nostalgically, momentarily seeing the youthful eyes of Viola searching his own.

"Well honey, there were a couple months there when it seemed you were hardly ever at home. I actually wondered if you were having an affair. Anyway, that's the first time it happened.

Around then, I mean." Flora smiled nervously and smoothed out some wrinkles in the bedcovers that didn't need smoothing.

Lucas felt a spike of anger in his gut and spoke without thinking. "But did you have to sleep with Chet's *son,* for God's sake? Did you stop to think how I might feel, all things considered? You know I thought it was Chet at first — I mean, before I saw who it was." Lucas was now speaking in an unmeasured rush, running way ahead of himself in a way that felt dangerous. He didn't want to upset his wife when her energy was so precious, but for once he couldn't seem to control himself. "I mean, is that it?" he seethed in a low tone, mindful of the minister downstairs. "Did you sleep with Pierre because he reminded you of Chet?"

Flora let a laugh escape her mouth, but immediately covered her lips so that another wouldn't follow. Then she smiled sadly at her husband and said, "For God's sake, Luke, no. I guess I slept with Pierre because he reminded me of *you.*" Lucas flinched visibly and Flora looked out the window with wet eyes for a moment before turning back to her husband, taking his hand and asking meekly, "I know this isn't fair and you don't even have to answer, Luke, but — did you ever have an affair?"

Lucas took a deep breath and eyed Flora straight on. "No, dear. Never."

Flora slid down to lay her head on her pillow again, closing her eyes with a contented smile. The wispy strands of the remaining hair that trailed from the scarf wrapped around her head were still flaming red against the pillow. "That's so nice," she cooed sleepily. "I know you're telling the truth, honey, because you couldn't lie to save your soul."

Flora died three days later. After several hours of choppy, labored breathing and bouts of delirium, she had finally seized up in a convulsion, choking, and by the time the nurse rushed to her she had collapsed against the pillow, ceasing to breathe. Wendy had been in the room for hours working crossword puzzles, her eyes flitting nervously toward her mom every few minutes. Pierre was there, sitting cross-legged on a chair, and Lucas had been standing for a long time with his arms folded, in a far corner of the room. When the moment of death came and went with surprising quickness, no one seemed to breathe for half a minute.

Then the nurse said softly, "That's it. God rest her loving soul," and Wendy dropped her book on the floor. Lucas walked over to place a hand on his daughter's shoulder, but she was just staring at the bed, silent as a stone.

It was Pierre who broke out in an anguished wail, leaning forward and cradling his head in his hands. "Oh Jesus," he wept, "*oh Jesus...*"

Lucas walked over to Pierre and softly tousled his dark hair. "It's all right son, it's all right," he said softly. "We'll make it somehow." In truth he didn't know how he was going to make it at all.

AS LUCAS entered his house with the entire 3RD Army seeming to hold its breath for miles around, he was smiling and shaking his head with a growing hilarity. As he suspected he would, he found Flora in the bedroom on her deathbed, her head rolling back and forth in delirium. The rest of the room was filled to the brim with a massive sound system, connected by a cord to the microphone that had fallen from Flora's hand to the floor. Lucas peered incredulously at the giant speakers pointed Pattonward and laughed, "This is too much. How do I come up with this stuff?" Then he bent down, got his arms under his wife's frail, cancer-ridden frame and lifted her gently into his arms.

As Flora looked into her husband's eyes with a bleary smile of recognition, Lucas smiled back and said, "Flora, whatever I ever said or implied about your playwriting, well, I apologize. I take it all back now. Because this scene —" he rolled his head to indicate everything, the room and the occupied city of Sacramento beyond — "is utterly *vacuous*."

Lucas was laughing again as he exited the house and bounded across the front lawn with his wife in his arms. "Hey General," he sang out, "here's the vicious enemy who was giving you such a pounding!"

Patton scrambled over the battlements and raced to meet the married couple. He stared quizzically at the limp woman in Lucas' arms and asked, "Is she dead?"

"Not yet," Lucas chuckled, "but she's getting there!"

"*Medic*!!" Patton bellowed, turning about-face to wave aggressively at the front line of troops behind him.

"That's okay, General," Lucas said matter-of-factly. "That won't be necessary." He abruptly up-ended Flora and stood her on her feet like a mannequin. "Upsy-daisy, there we go." Patton was scratching his head with a what-the-devil look. Lucas turned to Flora and said, "Flora, you've said ever since I got here that this is my show, right?"

"Thass right," Flora said unsteadily, still leaning against her husband for support.

"And I'm the writer, producer, and director?" he added.

Flora nodded her head sleepily in confirmation.

"Okay, then, fine," Lucas said with finality. "Don't take this personally, dear, but you look terrible." Lucas smartly snapped his fingers and Flora was transformed into the stunningly beautiful young woman he had met in college. Patton took a step back in surprise. Lucas looked over the general's battle-soiled uniform and commented, "And this is not the way I prefer to remember you either, sir." Another snap of the fingers and Patton was restored to his full-dress glory, a bright red ribbon choked with medals crossing over his chest and his starred helmet shining brightly in the sun.

"Why, thank you, son," the General beamed.

"Flora, meet General George S. Patton, commanding officer of the Third United States Army and military genius of the North African campaign and the Battle of the Bulge. As played by the Academy Award-winning actor George C. Scott, of course. General, sir, please meet my wife, the lovely and talented Flora Sanders Palmer of Alabama — as played by herself, of course. No one else could possibly fill that role."

"*Enchanté*," Patton chirped with a curt click of his heels, bussing Flora European-style on both her cheeks.

"Likewise, your honor," the young Flora retorted, grinning sarcastically. "I've heard too much about you."

"Now, now, none of that, Flo," Lucas chided. "The war is officially over. I'm declaring peace. I don't exactly know how all this works yet, but at least I know now that I'm in charge. And it's time to move on. The last I remember, my daughter really needed my help. I've got to get back down there — somehow — and have a real talk with her for a change."

There was an uncomfortable silence as Patton and Flora exchanged knowing looks, and Flora began shaking her head with pursed lips. "I'm sorry, dear," she finally said with a look of deep sympathy. "You've already written the ending. You can't change it now."

"What?!" Lucas whispered, stumbling backward a half-step.

"Buck up, son," Patton barked. "A man's gotta finish what he starts."

"What he starts?" Lucas repeated wonderingly. "But I didn't start anything. As I seem to recall, I had an accident!"

"Did you, Luke?" Flora asked in a kindly but corrective tone. "Was that really how all this came to pass? Try to remember, darling. Try to remember, one last time."

Chapter 20

LIKE three children filing into church, Wendy, Tom, and Cal stepped slowly into the curtained section of the ICU where Lucas Palmer lay comatose. Wendy gasped when she saw how besieged her father looked, his face no longer displaying the placid, otherworldly bluish cast of the day before. Though his eyes were closed and his features expressionless, the blotches of red and purple on his face and neck betrayed the recent struggle to restart his heart.

Dr. Chambers pointed out to Tom and Cal the heart monitor and two other machines that issued readouts of some sort, explaining their functions, but Wendy wasn't paying attention. As upset as she was by her father's appearance, she couldn't keep her eyes away from him. So much had happened to her in the last day, and particularly in the last few hours, that she felt he should know about. She almost wanted to thank him for starting the strange sequence of events that had begun the day before, but that would seem like a very peculiar, almost heartless thing to do. Certainly she couldn't mention the feeling to her companions, Dr. Chambers, or the nurse sitting attentively in the corner of the enclosure, reading a chart and adjusting dials on one of the mysterious machines. So Wendy kept it to herself as she intently watched her inert father and hoped against hope that at any moment he might awaken, speak her name, and rejoin the living.

LUCAS stepped back from his wife and the General and closed his eyes, stroking his forehead intently, trying to recall the last day he spent on earth. He could vaguely remember feeling depressed — deeply depressed, in fact, ever since Flora's death in 1995. His life thereafter had entered into a kind of limbo, a state of perpetual melancholy in which he clearly felt that the clock of his life was running down and could not be wound up again.

Chet had tried his best to lift his old friend's spirits, and even attempted to set him up with a series of blind dates in the company of himself and Stephanie, the new wife. But Lucas would sit through dinner dates with one female candidate after another hardly speaking, his mind always elsewhere and his heart suspended in a grievous traction.

Besides that, he was beginning to feel like a man twenty or thirty years beyond his own age, owing to a rapidly growing stiffness in his joints that sometimes made him feel half-frozen. He meant to go to a doctor to get checked out — could he be developing arthritis already? — but he just couldn't summon the initiative. When he would speak up on the dates arranged by Chet, it was often to complain about how stiff and crotchety he felt — not exactly a social lubricant, and sure as hell not an aphrodisiac. After a year or so, Chet gave up the attempts to fix Lucas' sad social life. He did make sure to invite Chet and Wendy along whenever he made trips to his new river house in Guerneville.

That was the connection, Lucas suddenly remembered —

the trip to Guerneville. If there was one thing that had focused his attention and revived an interest in life for Lucas, it was taking care of Wendy. Immediately after Flora's death he had panicked for a few days, aware that he had not the slightest idea of who his daughter really was or what she might need to kick-start her long-delayed life. But soon he decided that helping Wendy was the most immediate thing he could do to atone for a dubious career as a husband and father.

Lucas set about this work industriously. He made deliberate attempts to listen to Wendy's every word, to patiently absorb her whining and complaints and try to fathom, from the chaos and aimless indulgences of her daily life, where her talents and ambition might lie. Reverting to the excellent discipline of his undergraduate days, Lucas even started taking notes on their conversations. He didn't want to miss a clue to the mystery of his own daughter, anything she might inadvertently drop while they talked.

That technique had led directly to the recent Guerneville trip. During a repetition of Wendy's litany of complaints about Wayne Stoughton, the sleazy young salesman working under Chet's direction at Townsend Mercedes, Wendy had petulantly declared that she might as well become a lesbian. This was a new one for Lucas, and he had made a note of it. He even felt hopeful for Wendy; Stoughton was certainly no prize and perhaps she would be happier with a woman. When Lucas reread his scribble later, he immediately made a connection in his mind with the preponderance of gay couples, both male and female, that he had seen in Guerneville on the last trip there with Chet and Steph.

So Lucas had invited Wendy to Guerneville on the strength of the lesbian idea. But as the two of them walked down to the river just before lunchtime on that fateful Saturday, he already felt like a complete idiot. He didn't really think Wendy could meet anyone nice — female or male — in the space of a weekend that they would spend mostly in each other's company. What he had really meant to tell Wendy was that it might be good for them to get out of the house together, away from all the memories of Flora, and just have a truthful heart-to-heart. More than ever before, the ancient lie about Wendy's birth had been weighing on him; perhaps Flora had been right about the secret's negative effects on Wendy.

Instead Lucas had come up with the silly diversion of taking a rowboat out on the river. He knew this was another lame, out-of-touch notion when he reflected upon how phobic Wendy was about boats, airplanes, carnival rides, and automobile speeds above 30mph. The closest Wendy would get to the water was the end of the pier on the Townsends' property. Because the water pooled there like a small lake, Lucas thought it might appear safe enough to Wendy to lure her into the boat for at least a few minutes. When he had basically got the hang of using the oar, he started rowing in small circles about forty feet from Wendy's station on the pier, calling out to her about how much fun she was missing.

But she had steadfastly resisted him. Lucas eventually sank to the wooden-slat seat of the old flimsy boat in utter dejection. This wasn't working; nothing he tried with Wendy would ever work. He didn't know how to do this by himself. Without thinking he sank to his knees, turning to the side and holding the oar in front of him on the lip of the boat, bowing his head as if in prayer. "There must be another way," he said mournfully, looking out over the sparkling water. He recalled watching the dark green waves far beneath the Golden Gate Bridge, on the one day in his life he had considered suicide.

Now, looking at the river, Lucas wished mightily that he believed in some kind of helpful God, the way Flora always had. At that moment, any one of her densely populated pantheon of gods, goddesses, nature spirits and disembodied oracles of wisdom would have sufficed — anyone who could point the way to save his daughter from her vacant life and help him make sense of his own. He leaned harder on the oar resting on the lip of the rowboat, slightly tilting the side of the vessel down, and stared hard into the water until it seemed to ask him a wordless question.

"No, I would keep nothing for myself," he solemnly responded. Then he sat up with a jerk, wondering where that mysterious sentence had come from and what it could mean. He was getting as ditzy as Flora now; he'd better watch out for these encroaching signs of senility, particularly at the relatively tender age of fifty. Suddenly the oar slipped off the lip of the boat and flew out into the water. He had to reach far over the water to splash at the wooden tongue floating just beyond his reach. The boat was beginning to rock ever more unsteadily.

"Da-ad?" came Wendy's voice from the pier as Lucas got a grip on the paddle, and pulled it back to the boat.

"I think I've just about got the hang of this thing!" he yelled with a false gaiety, hoisting the dripping oar high into the air. Wendy was waving at him, mumbling something he couldn't hear. Steadying the boat, he slipped the oar into the water and paddled a few feet closer to the pier. "What did you say, honey?"

"I said, *Write home real soon!*" she shouted. Lucas laughed ruefully and waved her off, then glimpsed something strange and brilliant, like the flash of a huge diamond, in the bottom of the boat. He dropped to his knees again to look closer, but

but could find nothing. When he tried to regain the seat behind him his left hip joint froze up, a searing pain shot from his groin to his left big toe, and he wrenched violently into a half-standing position in response.

"*Oh, shit!*" Lucas exclaimed as the boat rocked wildly, throwing him off balance as his legs tangled underneath him. He glimpsed the lip of the boat and the sun-blessed water of the river rushing at him for just an instant before his head was cruelly jarred into blackness.

"Oh my," Lucas said thoughtfully as he opened his eyes to find Flora and General Patton gazing at him with the same curious kindness in their eyes. "Does this mean…?"

"That's right, honey," Flora asserted. "Prayers do get answered, even when we don't know that we're making them. And prayers made with such purity of spirit — well honey, that one was a real doozy."

"A very daring initiative," Patton added with military precision. "I'm honored to have served with you on this historic…"

Lucas cut off the General and advanced on Flora to press a serious question. "But what about Wendy?" he asked. "What's going to happen if I can't go back to help Wendy?"

Flora smiled broadly and said, "Luke, dear, have a little faith in your own works. Wendy's doing just fine. She has new friends, some new feelings, and even some new clothes, for goodness' sake. Listen, dear, if it'll make you feel better, why don't you just have a look yourself?"

From behind her back Flora produced the short wand she had been holding when Lucas first arrived in the otherworld. She used it to point Lucas' attention behind himself. He whipped around and saw a circular lens hanging in midair, just like the one he had looked through when his recent incredible journey had begun. When he peered into the lens he could see a miniature but discernible camera's-eye view of a hospital scene, populated by five people arranged around a bed in which a man lay unmoving.

Lucas could see a beefy black doctor with a white jacket, a tall man and a short man, a nurse sitting at one corner of the bed, and his daughter Wendy in an unfamiliar, curly hairdo and an even more unfamiliar but elegant pantsuit. She looked like a sophisticated young woman, not the petulant, overgrown child he had grown so used to seeing over the years. The scene he was watching seemed to have no audio feed, so he could discern nothing that was actually happening. Yet what he was watching made him unreasonably happy nonetheless.

"And not only that," Flora whispered at Lucas' shoulder, her arms wrapping around him from behind, "she's going to help a doctor who needs her. A very important doctor, I might add. Who *really* needs her, I might also add."

"Oh yeah?" Lucas responded giddily, his spirits soaring higher than he had felt in many years. "Well, that's just great!" He leaned over toward the suspended lens and cupped a hand by his mouth, shouting down toward the earthly scene, "Hey, Wendy!"

"Daddy?!" Wendy shrieked, clutching the bed rails and leaning far over the center of the bed, her body lunging at her father's.

"Wendy!" Cal exclaimed, and reached out to grab her back. She twisted in his sudden embrace and said, "Didn't you hear him, Cal? He just said my name!"

Cal looked at Wendy worriedly, shaking his head as she twisted again to face Tom. "Tom, you heard him, didn't you? My dad just said, 'Hey Wendy!'" But Tom only shrugged his shoulders, looking for the first time as if he couldn't understand the inexplicable. Wendy shook her head vigorously and ran a hand through her stylishly poofed hair, muttering "I could swear I heard…"

Three violent beeps rang out in the curtained enclosure, replaced quickly by a high-toned whining. All eyes turned to the heart monitor that showed Lucas Palmer flatlining. "Out! Out! Everybody **OUT** of here!" Dr. Chambers bellowed, roughly shoving Tom out of his way and expertly dropping the rails on one side of the bed. Tom stumbled into Cal and Wendy, and they all started falling over like a clump of Keystone Cops, just barely regaining their footing in time to avoid hitting the floor as their momentum carried them into the central area of the ICU. A gaggle of nurses was rushing past them with a wheeled machine as Chambers shouted instructions in the background. One nurse stopped in her tracks to urgently point the way out of the ICU to the stumbling trio.

Lucas watched the chaotic scene with intense interest until it faded to black and the lens vanished. He turned slowly around in Flora's embrace and said thoughtfully, "So that's it? The final curtain? Is that all she… I mean, all I wrote?"

"Almost, dear," Flora replied, reaching up to kiss him on the cheek. "Time is running short now. We have to get going."

Lucas was about to ask exactly where they should get going to when he noticed General Patton standing right next to him, grinning from ear to ear and jutting his chin into the air, as jaunty as a rooster. "General Patton," Lucas said warmly as he proffered his right hand in friendship, "I presume you won't be going with us. What becomes of an old soldier like yourself?"

"Oh, don't worry about me, sonny. As long as people come here with an inner war raging — and most of 'em do, the poor dumb bastards — I can always be conjured to serve." Patton refused the hand of Lucas, instead drawing himself up to his full height and raising the blade of his hand to his helmet in salute. "Sir," he added solemnly.

IN THE main lobby of the hospital, an impromptu postmortem was going on twenty minutes after Dr. Chambers' last attempt to revive Lucas Palmer had failed. Tom was sitting with an arm around Wendy, who sat dry-eyed with a mysterious smile on her face listening to Dr. Chambers sorrowfully explain why Lucas' condition had proved too serious to save him.

"Of course I couldn't say this when you arrived here yesterday, Miss Palmer, but I knew from the moment I saw your dad that he couldn't make it. After a while, you just know the look of death when it's so close by — I'm sorry, Miss Palmer, perhaps that's a terrible thing to say."

"Wendy," replied Wendy softly. "Please just call me Wendy."

"Sure, uh, Wendy," the doctor acceded. "May I say how well you seem to be taking all this? You're quite composed for someone in this kind of situation."

Wendy gazed at the doctor and realized with a sudden thrill that he was absolutely right. She was not only composed at the most unlikely moment — she was composed, period. She couldn't remember the last time she had felt that way. "Oh, don't worry about me, Dr. Chambers," she said girlishly. "I'll break down and have a real fit before too long. Just you wait and see."

"Horace," the doctor replied softly. "Just call me Horace."

He tilted his head to one side and nodded toward Cal, sitting off by himself on a lounge chair and staring straight ahead with tear-filled eyes. "Is he going to be all right?"

Wendy bolted from Tom's arm and almost bowled over Horace Chambers in her rush to get to Cal's side. She had never seen him crying before. She sat on a low table next to him and said gently, "Cal? Are you okay?"

Cal turned his head mournfully toward Wendy and whimpered, "I didn't save him. I couldn't swim fast enough…"

"Oh honey, now stop that," Wendy cooed, drawing Cal's head toward her generous bosom and twisting her head back to give Tom a raised-eyebrows look.

"**HEY** now," Chambers intervened righteously, "**YOU** gave him the only chance he **HAD**, Mr. Davidson. "There was nothing **MORE** you could have **DONE**."

"That's right, Cal," Tom called from his seat. There was a sudden commotion at the hospital entrance. A silver-haired Chet Townsend rushed into the lobby with such force that he literally skidded to a stop when he came abreast of Wendy holding the softly weeping Cal.

"Wendy!" Chet bellowed. "I got your friend's message when I opened the shop and I've been hell for leather getting down here since. Where's Luke, for God's sake? Is he all right?"

Startled, Wendy could only stare blankly at Chet and mutely shake her head. Chambers rose from his seat and clapped Chet on the shoulder. "Sir, I am Dr. Chambers, the attending physician here. I'm afraid Mr. Palmer passed away about a half hour ago. He was in a very deep coma for the last twenty-four hours. He had a serious concussion and he took in a lot of water in the accident yesterday. I'm sorry, there was just no way we could pull him out of it."

Chet Townsend spun around once, as slow and awkward as a dancing bear, causing Chambers to reach out and steady him, guiding him toward the nearest empty lounge chair. "Well, fuck me," Chet cursed as he dropped heavily into the soft upholstery. "*Fuck me*. My best friend is gone and I didn't even get to say good-bye."

"I'm very sorry for your loss, Mister..." Chambers responded gently.

"Townsend," Chet replied, reaching one hand up toward the doctor without leaving his chair. "Chet Townsend, Townsend Mercedes of Sacramento." Chambers reached forward and took Chet's firm grip, casting a bemused look at Wendy. Chet held onto the doctor's hand a full ten seconds, squeezing him mightily and looking as if he might explode at any moment. He released the black man's hand before speaking again.

"Man was a goddamn hero, did you know that, Doctor? He didn't say much and I guess not many people knew him, but he was a goddamn hero. The things he did to keep his family together, the things he endured..."

Chet leaned forward and shook a finger at Wendy. "And the things he did for you, missy, I hope you won't forget. Do you know he could hardly talk about anything else for the last few years, ever since your mother died? Never seen a man so devoted to a child as your dad was to you, Wendy. Man was a real hero. What a loss. What a goddamn loss."

Fifteen minutes later, the scene in the hospital lobby had rearranged itself into a tableau of farewells. Cal had dried his eyes and was standing with Tom near the exit, waiting for Wendy to extricate herself from Chet Townsend's embrace. The big man was standing with one arm around her shoulder, pointing a finger in her face again. Horace Chambers stood a few feet away behind Chet and Wendy, waiting on something unknown.

"Anything you need, Wendy, you just give me a call," Chet

was booming, his composure having fully rebounded into a take-charge attitude. "From now on you can consider yourself a part of my family. You shall not want for anything, and I mean that. That's the least I can do in the memory of your dad. You hear me? I mean it now, missy."

Wendy shot a help-me look toward Tom and Cal, then tried to negotiate an escape on her own. "That's so nice of you, Mr. Townsend, and I'm sure I can use your help in the next few days, with the funeral and all that. After that, I guess I've got to sort things out for myself, you know?"

"You don't wait one second to call me," Chet insisted. "You call me for anything you need, you understand?"

Wendy nodded violently, hoping that the bigness of the movement would convince Chet she meant to comply. Horace Chambers glanced nervously at his watch and finally stepped around Chet Townsend to thrust a business card at Wendy. His voice was soft, childlike, nervous. "Look, Wendy, I'm sorry we met under these terrible circumstances but I — well, we try to do follow-up on all our patients here, I mean, on the ones that are still living anyway... What I mean is, anything you need to call me about, feel free. There's my card." As soon as Wendy took it, nodding and smiling, the doctor nervously turned about and disappeared down the hallway into the depths of the hospital.

Chet shook Wendy once more with his big arm around her and then stepped back, whistling with admiration. "Say, Wendy, you're looking pretty sharp these days. Did you do something with your hair?"

Fifteen feet away, Tom slapped the back of his hand against Cal's chest and whispered fervently, "*Oh my God.*"

"What? What?" Cal responded, looking around him in

every direction.

Tom pointed surreptitiously at Chet and Wendy. "Don't you *see*? Oh, my God."

Cal put his arm around Tom's shoulder and whispered back with an equal urgency. "No, I do not see anything. And I do not *want* to see anything. And whatever it is you're seeing, perhaps you would be wise to keep it to yourself. Not everybody has to know everything about everybody, Tom. Some secrets should be kept."

"Okay, okay," Tom replied hastily, cowering. "I mean, maybe I'm wrong. I could be wrong — but if you look..."

"I'm not *listening!*" Cal sang out, placing both hands over his ears and heading for the automatic doors of the hospital.

LUCAS was sitting with Flora again on a hillside in the gorgeous "real world" where she had first reappeared to him as the beautiful young woman who was restored to him now. He looked happily about at the scene which seemed whole and utterly genuine again, and asked like a child, "So if everything is forgiven here, will we stay together forever?"

Flora laughed casually and replied, "No, honey, it doesn't work that way. Remember that I told you this is just a waystation? Where we're headed, there is no world at all — and we won't be ourselves anymore. Who we've been, what we've done, none of that will matter. We'll be joining in, just like raindrops falling in a river. It's hard to explain. But I know we'll understand everything when we get there."

Lucas sighed, obviously disappointed but still game for whatever happened next. "Lucas Palmer," he said as if were reading a subject title on the cover of a *National Geographic*. "So much for him, huh? I guess he's no great loss to the world."

Flora's response could have been taken as an insult, but the faraway tone in which she said the words suggested another meaning entirely. "No loss at all, honey," she murmured. "There is no loss."

Lucas bit his lower lip and nodded his head, picking idly at the grass. "I see," he said, then added, "Look, Flora, there's just one more thing I've got to do. Do we have any time? Can I still write something in?"

"Sure, honey," Flora answered indulgently, as if she knew what he was up to. "Just don't leave me here too long. You know how lonely I get."

"Thanks, dear," Lucas said, giving his wife a kiss on the cheek and standing up to snap his fingers. In a split second he was hovering over the earth at a distance of about twenty miles, taking an affectionate look at the great green and blue orb he had spent a lifetime mapping and describing to his students without ever getting a feel for the wholeness, the innate sense of the planet.

Now that he had one last chance to conduct an unlimited survey, he wanted to settle a lingering curiosity. He wanted to circle the globe in eighty ways, get an unprecedented view from the top, finally see the whole in the fragments. Once he had done that, he felt sure he could put together a grand universal theory: a meta-geography. With a grand smile he took one magnificent step, covering miles in its dizzying span, and then another and another. With every step Lucas discovered that he could move higher, faster, farther — and soon, he was flying.

ABOUT FEARLESS BOOKS

FEARLESS BOOKS was founded by author D. Patrick Miller in 1997 to keep his work in print after several misadventures with major New York publishers. It has since grown into a diverse literary agency, offering professional representation, manuscript editing and development, and assisted publishing services to hundreds of independent working writers. Information about those services is available at *www.fearlessbooks.com*.

Miller's own work, including his books, journalism reports & essays, poetry, and photography can be viewed at his personal writing site, *www.dpatrickmiller.com*.

Made in the USA
Middletown, DE
07 September 2022